For My Cousins

MERE JOYCE

THINGS THAT FALL

DCB

Canada Council
for the Arts
Conseil des Arts
du Canada
 ONTARIO ARTS COUNCIL
CONSEIL DES ARTS DE L'ONTARIO
an Ontario government agency
un organisme du gouvernement de l'Ontario

 ONTARIO | ONTARIO
CREATES | CRÉATIF
Canadian
Heritage
Patrimoine
canadien
 Canada

The publisher gratefully acknowledges the support of the Canada Council for the Arts and
the Ontario Arts Council for its publishing program. We acknowledge the financial support
of the Government of Canada through the Canada Book Fund (CBF) for our publishing
activities, and the Government of Ontario through Ontario Creates, an agency of the
Ontario Ministry of Culture, and the Ontario Book Publishing Tax Credit Program.

LIBRARY AND ARCHIVES CANADA CATALOGUING IN PUBLICATION

Title: Things that fall / Mere Joyce.
Names: Joyce, Mere, 1988– author.
Identifiers: Canadiana (print) 20190089636 |
Canadiana (ebook) 20190089644 |
ISBN 9781770865563 (softcover) | ISBN 9781770865570 (html)
Classification: LCC PS8619.O975 T55 2019 | DDC JC813/.6—DC23

United States Library of Congress Control Number: 2018967102

Cover design: Angel Guerra
Interior text design: tannicegdesigns.ca

Printed and bound in Canada
Manufactured by Houghton Boston Printers in
Saskatoon, Saskatchewan, Canada in August 2019.

DCB
AN IMPRINT OF CORMORANT BOOKS INC.
260 SPADINA AVENUE, SUITE 502, TORONTO, ONTARIO, M5T 2E4
www.dcbyoungreaders.com
www.cormorantbooks.com

KAYLA

THE WINDOW IS MOCKING me.

High up on the wall and small, not much larger than the narrow panes built into new home basements, its shine a taunting reminder of the bright October day waiting outside this dismal parlor.

I blink away from the hint of sun and glance over to where Mom and Dad stand talking to some bald guy I don't know. I should be the dutiful daughter and join in the conversation. I don't want to risk disappointing my parents, but I'm also not eager to leave my comfortable spot. We came early, and I nabbed a corner angled away from the casket at the far end of the room. Prime real estate in an awful place like this. When more people start showing up, I'll lose it for sure.

Stuck with indecision, I stay rooted as my eyes stray toward a couple standing near the coffin I can't quite see. The people are unfamiliar, and I watch their somber poses until they step away to make room for others. When their rigid forms no longer totally obscure my view of the casket, my gaze snaps back to the rectangle of light from the window. I saw the body when I first arrived. I have no interest in spending more time staring at it.

Why do people insist on having corpses present at a funeral? Wouldn't everyone feel more at ease without the dead body dressed up like a demented life-sized doll?

The room is quiet, and even from its far side I hear snippets of my parents' conversation.

"It wasn't just Simon," the bald guy scoffs in response to some comment my dad has made. "Growing up I spent more time with the Hacher family than I did my own."

The sound of my uncle's name as I gaze at the small rectangle of light sends a tingle of annoyance through me — the same kind of frustration I felt on Tuesday when I sat in math class, trying hard to focus on the equations in my textbook instead of the streaming sun beyond the windowpane. That was four days ago, when I was still oblivious to the fact that at the same moment I was watching a bird flitting by on the other side of the glass, Uncle Simon was miles away, lifting a load of plywood in the above-average September heat — and collapsing beneath its weight as his heart gave out.

Four days ago. For four days, my uncle has been dead. And now I'm here, wasting a warm, yellow Saturday in a room black with mourning.

"After all," the guy continues, "the cooking was always better, and at my house I was surrounded by girls."

Dad laughs, and I tilt my chin in his direction, curious about his reaction. My father doesn't talk about his brothers. He hasn't even seen any of them in a decade, Uncle Simon's body notwithstanding.

"Joey and Oscar would have loved to switch places with me," the guy says, referencing two of the four brothers Dad never mentions at home. "Quite a change from a house of five boys to one with three girls. Those two loved my sisters. A little too much, if you recall."

The guy — who must be an old family friend my parents have never bothered to mention — smiles, before his expression falls.

"Simon loved them, too, but not in the same way," he adds. "He just thought it was spectacular to have a girl around."

He gives Dad a weird look then, a glance clearly meant to convey something important. Dad's quick to avert his gaze, which makes me uneasy. I turn back to the window, wishing I weren't standing here alone. If only Hudson had been able to come home for the weekend — my boyfriend would be a much better distraction than the irritating pane of light.

"Kayla?"

Footsteps sound behind me, and I turn to find a different source of distraction as someone stares at me from the back of the parlor. For half a second, I wonder who the girl is. When I finally recognize her face, I'm washed with embarrassment — and a grateful sense of oncoming respite.

Hailey.

My cousin, half a year older than I am, stands with her family near the room's entrance. I haven't seen Hailey since we were seven years old. And yet, I know both her and the younger siblings standing at her sides, a boy and a girl I haven't seen since one was a toddler and the other one a babe. They're strangers, but I know them all.

How can people be so familiar and at the same time so completely unknown?

My uncle Dean hovers near the entryway with his family, my aunt beside him, the kids a step behind. They look drained and uncertain, like my own parents did four days ago when they got the phone call from the hospital where Dad had been listed as next of kin.

Uncle Dean's eyes scan the room until they find his dead brother's body. I watch him sob, holding a fist to his mouth as he turns in against his wife's embrace.

Then I look away.

My eyes veer to where Dad stands watching his brother, unmoving. The sight is disturbing. I wonder if my dad will eventually cross the room or if he'll spend the entire morning studying Dean from afar.

Saying I don't know much about the history of Dad's family fight is a blatant lie. I know nothing about it, except it means Dad hasn't spoken to any of his four brothers in ten years. And now there's one brother he'll never be able to speak to again.

Hailey ushers her younger siblings away from their parents, and

I look back in time to see them approaching me. I smile, relieved to have her nearby. Maybe I don't know Hailey anymore, but at one time we were close, the two of us part of a cluster of cousins our parents used to call the Group of Seven. Besides, having someone around my age — someone holding the same position as "niece to the deceased" — means a lot in a situation like this.

"Hey," I murmur, my voice rising only a fraction above a whisper. Everything I've said this morning has been quiet. A normal tone seems disrespectful here.

"Hi," Hailey sighs, leaning forward and pulling me into an unexpected hug. As soon as she envelops me, though, I remember Hailey has always hugged people. The recollection is amusing, and her weight against me is a comfort. She smells like eucalyptus and cedar wood. I breathe in the earthy scents and let myself enjoy the familiarity of the moment.

When Hailey steps back, she runs her fingers through her hair. The strands are thick, black, and long, a complete difference from the thin, mousy mane covering my head. Hailey's mother is Cree, and Hailey looks far more like her mother now than she ever did when we were children. She's grown into her heritage, and the result is stunning. Her skin is darker than mine, her brown eyes bright and wide, her small lips a crooked heart. Our fathers are brothers, and I look like my dad, but no one would ever think Hailey and I were related. She's taller than me, and her frame is fuller, her curves more pronounced. I don't consider myself a beast, but without self-pity I can admit Hailey is prettier than I am. She has a natural kind of beauty I don't possess. I don't even think she's wearing makeup, and still her features are more radiant than my carefully contoured ones.

Her sister is like her miniature twin, while her brother has more of his father's looks, his hair lighter and short, his eyes blue and his face round. After Hailey's hugged me, she takes a moment to guide them to a couple of nearby chairs that are out of view of the casket.

Her sister whispers something, and Hailey glances back at me with a frown.

"She's your cousin," Hailey explains to the little girl, who must not even remember who I am.

The description feels odd, like it has smacked my funny bone and left an uncomfortable prickle shaking down my arm. Maybe if I lived across the country from these kids it wouldn't be weird for them not to know me. But we're only an hour away from each other. Or, at least, we used to be. It's not unheard of for people to move in the space of a decade, so it's possible Hailey's family has relocated.

The uncertainty of it all makes me squirm. Should cousins need to behave like strangers?

Hailey hands her sister a cellphone and warns her to keep the volume off as the two kids hunch over the screen to play a game. They look uncomfortable, crowding so close together they're practically sharing a single chair. I wonder why their parents even made them come.

Hailey waits until the two are settled before she turns back to me with another sigh.

"Crazy, eh?" she says, nodding her head in the direction of our late uncle. "And to think of all that time wasted. My dad hadn't seen him in years. Stupid men."

Her words cause an instant reflex in my muscles. I grab her arm, my nails pressing into her blouse.

"Your dad hadn't seen him, either?" I ask. This is not news I anticipated hearing. Of all the people in attendance today, I believed only my parents and I would be the outsiders skirting the edges of my late uncle's life. "It wasn't just my dad who stopped speaking to the family? I figured everyone else still saw each other."

My cousin's startled expression probably matches my own.

"No. At least, not my dad," she says. "I don't think he's talked to any of his brothers in, I don't know …"

"Ten years?" I interject.

Hailey glances at her parents with a nod.

"Yeah, I guess that's about right," she says. "You too?"

I relax my grip and let my fingers slide off her arm.

"Me too."

"Shit," Hailey mumbles, sighing for the third time since her arrival.

My cousin and I stand together, watching groups of people enter the parlor. I don't know any of them. I suppose they're friends, co-workers, or maybe relatives from Aunt Shirley's side of the family. Whoever they are, their appearance is dull and stiff as they enter the long red-carpeted and beige-walled room.

I can't get my head around the choice of venue. My uncle doesn't fit in a place like this — he never liked being cooped up inside. I have faded visions of him swimming at the bay in summer, pushing our sleds down snow-packed hills in winter, and even guiding us through an endless corn maze at Halloween. But I can't remember him ever in a suit or in a dreary building like this surrounded by such an unhappy group of people.

I lean into Hailey, and she doesn't hesitate to lean right back in against me.

"Where do you think Aunt Shirley is?" she asks after a minute, her voice low. "And Forrester? Damn, I can't imagine what he's going through."

"I've been thinking about that for days," I mumble, scanning the room even though I know our cousin isn't here. When Dad got the call from the hospital, he asked where his brother's wife was, but he's been tight-lipped about whatever answer he received. Simon must have had a reason for listing his oldest brother as next of kin over his wife. As it is, I haven't seen Shirley *or* her son.

Forrester is a year older than Hailey and I, and for him, this isn't just some melancholy function. He's lost his dad. At the age of eighteen.

My stomach lurches with the thought.

"Come on, there's Thomas and Nolan."

Hailey's words break through the sickness, and I twist my head to try to locate the new arrivals. Before I can set my sights on our other cousins — two more members of our old playmate group — Hailey is pulling me across the room to greet them. When I do spot them, however, there's no half-second of incomprehension. The recognition is immediate. The older brother of nineteen and the younger sixteen-year-old are both tall and skinny, attributes carried over from the days of our childhood. They each share a strong resemblance to their dad as well — they are definitely Hacher family boys.

The sides of Thomas's head are shaved, his brown hair gelled into a flat strip on the top. He wears small gauges in each ear and a hooped ring in his left helix, and on the inside of his wrists the edges of tattoos peek out from the cuffs of his suit jacket. Nolan's got the same brown hair, though his is loose, bordering on unruly. He's also gone for a simpler fashion statement. No piercings or tattoos that I can see, and nothing on his outfit to suggest his mom didn't buy it for him at a generic department store.

He's got a few years to catch up with his brother, though I wonder if he'll ever copy the same style. As kids, Thomas was always robust in his attitude, while Nolan was the quietest of us all. To judge them in the shallowest form now, I'd say their appearances suggest those qualities may have lingered.

Of course, judging them at all is ludicrous. Having to guess at the personality of two boys I used to know better than even my own brother is pathetic. But at least we're not standing in silence, avoiding each other like our parents.

The arrival of Thomas and Nolan brings our reunited circle up to four. Only three of us are left before the Group of Seven is complete. When I got up this morning, I didn't give any thought to my relatives, beyond Uncle Simon and Forrester. Now, desperation sparks in my nerves, hot and unexpected. I want the others to make their appearance so I can see how they've grown and guess at how they've changed. The last time the entire family was together, such a long time ago, the seven of us would have been side by side. I'd like to experience that again, even if only to cement this day as a day of separation as we say the goodbyes we never got as kids.

NOLAN

MY PHONE BUZZES WITHIN ten seconds of walking inside the drab building. Which is a relief. I had the notion I'd be stepping into a parallel universe when we got here. Knowing a text is awaiting my reply is so damn normal it keeps me settled in reality.

B: How is it?

I just have time to read the message before Thomas nudges a warning for me to put my phone away. Fair enough. Places like this must have their own set of unwritten rules. No texting when a cadaver's nearby probably ranks high on the list.

Our uncle has the terrible honor of being the first dead body I've ever seen. All things considered, I'm pretty lucky for that. I remember the week two years ago when Thomas disappeared, and I kept dreaming I'd have to identify his body at the morgue. But those were only dreams, ones that ended seven days later when my brother stepped into our front hall — alive and well after an impromptu camping trip with his buddies.

I haven't had nightmares like that in two years. And this is different, anyway. As vivid as my dreams were, they don't compare to the physical reality of the body now across the room. A body I should know, but one that carries only a vague resemblance to the uncle I hardly remember.

I peel my gaze from the corpse and instead focus on the two girls headed our way. I'm already preparing to cringe at the oncoming onslaught of Thomas's well-practiced flirtation strategy before I realize they're my cousins. Which is even weirder than seeing Uncle Simon in a coffin. Less because I figured my brother would hit on them and more because these girls are old enough — strange enough — to be potential targets of his flirting obsession.

"What is this all about?" Hailey smirks, stepping toward us and giving Thomas's confused style of formal attire and punkish adornments a dubious once-over.

"Wanted to look spiffy for you, darling cousin," he replies with joyful sarcasm.

She walks up to him, and he pulls her into a hug, the two of them moving like actors used to blocking a scene. Thomas, of course, would say the motion was not rehearsed but rather automatic, a natural reaction to having her close. He presses her tightly to his chest and then gives her long hair a tug as he plants a kiss on her forehead. The mere suggestion of flirtation seems inexcusable now. Their behavior in this moment radiates family tenderness.

I'm jealous of how easy they are together. I'm anything but at ease here, and I don't know these girls. If I saw them on the street, I would walk by without a second glance.

Or, maybe that's not entirely true. Hailey's got soft hair and mature features, but her smile is familiar, even if her body is not. Like the text message buzzing against my leg, it makes all of this feel more real.

Of course, I'm not sure "real" is good today. But that's beside the point.

Hailey moves out of my brother's embrace and offers me a gentler squeeze.

"And how are you?" she asks.

I shrug, giving her the small smile Thomas assures me would be better utilized by him. He may have the stronger social skills, but Thomas likes to tell me the landscape of my face is so charming it's ridiculous. I'm not sure my smile is as swoon-worthy as he seems to think, but I'll give it to him that he's far better suited to the birthmark on my neck. My brother used to tell me it was a scar from being slashed at knifepoint when I was a baby. If the mark graced his neck instead of mine, Thomas would undoubtedly use a similar story now at every party he attended.

"I'm fine," I mumble, glancing down to where another message announces its arrival inside my pocket. Before the temptation to check my phone grows, I focus on our other cousin. "Hey, Kayla."

"Hey, Nolan," she replies, stepping close but not going so far as to throw her arms around me. "Hey, Thomas."

"Sucks about Simon, doesn't it?" Thomas says, looping an arm around Kayla's shoulder and bringing her in to his side. Even from here I get a whiff of the coconut she must use in her shampoo. The scent is strong, but nice.

"No kidding," Hailey scoffs. "All of this … it's so bizarre."

"What, being at our uncle's funeral, or being at our uncle's funeral when we haven't even seen him since we were kids?" Thomas asks.

Hailey and Kayla exchange a glance that suggests it's been just as long for them, too. I'm not surprised by the information, even if it is unexpected. My father's not the type to single-handedly piss off his entire family. Makes more sense it was a joint effort. From what I remember and the stories Thomas has shared, Dad used to do everything with his brothers. Seems appropriate even their falling-out was a family affair.

Across the room, Dad now stands against the back wall talking to someone I've never met, his eyes snaking over to his brothers every few seconds. None of them are talking to one another. Five brothers make up the Hacher family. Four of them are now in the same room — three of them unwilling to communicate, and one unable to.

Seven days was too long to go without talking to Thomas. I don't want to imagine ten years without my brother in my life.

"Do you think the twins will be here?" Kayla asks.

Uncle Joey is the last Hacher brother missing. Allison and Eli, the twins, are his kids.

"They'll be here," Thomas replies.

"Have you talked to them?" Hailey asks.

He shakes his head, while I make an unsuccessful attempt to remember the last time I talked to the twins or their parents.

"Nope. But Joey wouldn't miss his brother's funeral," Thomas says. "No way would he do that."

My gaze shifts to the door, where a new quartet is entering the macabre scene.

"Looks like you're right," I say, nodding toward the entrance.

The timing of their arrival is impeccable, and the on-cue moment would be perfect if the family didn't look so awkward as they slink into the room. Allison, Eli, and their parents join the solemn crowd, their expressions hardened and their steps unsure.

When Allison sees us, her wary look softens into something like relieved annoyance — as if she's glad we're here, but pissed off she and Eli are the last ones to arrive. She grabs her brother by the sleeve and drags him along to join our little club.

"What a way to see each other," she says in greeting.

Her skin is red with blemishes, and her blond hair is scraped back into a scalp-tight bun. I'm used to people saying Thomas and I look the same. We're equal in height and build, and our features are similar enough it's obvious we're brothers. But I'd be quick to call Allison and Eli identical, if that weren't impossible.

My memory is unquestionably fuzzy, but according to the collected photographs adorning the side cupboard in our family room, Allison once had a penchant for frilly dresses. And I *do* remember being impressed by Eli's wide array of superhero shirts. Now they've both veered into less specific styles. Not only do they share the same shapeless frame, they also have the same spotted skin, thick lips, and blue eyes.

Even their outfits are alike. Black shoes, black pants, black shirts. They're like a matching pair of waiters. If it weren't for Allison's bun differing from her brother's shorter, shaggy haircut, it'd be easy to assume they were both one gender or the other.

"Yeah, but there's still one of us missing," Thomas sighs in answer to Allison's remark.

"Forrester." Kayla nods.

The six of us fall into silence as we each search for a glimpse of our other cousin, but he's not here. Neither is his mom. Maybe they're off somewhere together, mourning in private.

With none of us speaking, it's easy to listen to the murmurs surrounding us as everyone shares their stories of our uncle's life. Near the coffin, someone cries. Away from the coffin, my parents now stand together, both of them staring at the floor.

Reality is slipping away again. I wish my phone would vibrate with another text.

"They're not talking. None of them are talking," Hailey comments after a while, snatching the thought right out of my brain. "It's sick."

"They're grieving," Allison says.

"Yep," Thomas says, unable to keep the edge of annoyance out of his voice. "They're grieving. And they should be doing it together."

"Have any of them talked to each other lately? At all?" Kayla looks between us, and we all share the same lost expression.

"I don't think so," I say.

"It's sick," Hailey mumbles again, leaning her head against Kayla's shoulder.

"What do you say we go outside for a while?" Thomas suggests, his fingers straying up to twist one of the gauges in his right ear. "I don't think I can stay in here much longer."

"Sounds like a good idea to me," Hailey agrees. She grabs Kayla's arm and leads the way toward the exit.

We leave the room together, the six of us uninterrupted as we walk past our four sets of parents. I feel a bit bad I didn't go to the coffin to pay my respects, but I don't really need to stand over my uncle's body to say a final goodbye. Not while all around him his brothers stand in silence.

The sun outside is bright, the air warm and fresh after the staleness of the funeral home. Summer returned to Ontario last week, and its refusal to surrender to fall would be glorious if the circumstances weren't so grim. We set our sights on the park across the street, waiting for a few cars to pass on the road — the drivers craning their necks at the sight of six teens dressed in mourning attire — before we cross.

I stand at the back of the group, letting the others check for traffic as I peek at my phone. Two new messages have appeared in the time I've been inside, joining the first on my phone's preview screen.

B: How is it?

B: Call me when you're done.

B: I probably shouldn't be texting you
   right now, should I? Sorry for being
   a disrespectful ass.

I smile, sliding the phone back into my pocket as we cross the street.

The pavement gives way to hard-packed dirt and grass as we walk to the picnic area where tables are spread across a flat field beside a playground. Someone sits on top of the closest table, his broad shoulders clad in a navy collared shirt. The sight of the slumped figure is, like everything else today, surreal, a mixture of odd recognition and absurd unfamiliarity.

"Hey, Forrester," Thomas says when we're close enough.

Forrester glances up, first at my brother, then at us all. His blank expression changes to one of amusement. Amusement, tucked away under mounds of pain.

Allison is right. After all these years, this is one hell of a way for us to reunite.

HAILEY

FORRESTER LOOKS LIKE SHIT.

I haven't seen the boy in forever, but it doesn't take a genius to realize the almost black bags under his bloodshot brown eyes aren't part of his usual getup. Of course, it also doesn't take a genius to guess losing your dad can have that kind of effect.

What a crazy-ass way for us to meet up again. Kayla said it's been ten years. Sounds about right. But damn, ten years is way too long.

I used to think about my cousins a lot when I was a kid. Years after I'd last seen them, I remember asking my parents if I could call Kayla or go to Thomas and Nolan's house. My mother said we were too busy, or Dad claimed they were unavailable. I knew they were lying, but back then I was so dim-witted it never occurred to me I could look up their numbers — hell, even look them up online — and contact them myself.

I guess I stopped thinking about them when I started high school, when my life was first commandeered by homework, parties, and hot boys. But while I was forgetting, my cousins were growing up. Long after I mostly forgot, one of them lost his dad.

Forrester looks like shit, and it's a good representation of how I'm feeling right now, too.

"Glad someone finally found me," Forrester says, as the rest of us assemble around the picnic table. "I was starting to think no one remembered I exist."

There's no need to question why he stayed outside. We're idiots if we can't figure it out, and no one here is going to make him explain the all-too-fucking-obvious.

"Where's your mom?" Kayla asks instead.

Forrester licks his lips. They're cracked, probably like everything else in his life right now.

"Not coming," he mumbles, trying to hide the tremble in his voice. I start to say something but clamp my jaw shut before the choice words bouncing on my thick tongue tumble out. I'm good at running my mouth, but right now it might be better if someone less inclined to spout expletives voices their opinion first.

My eyes shift to Thomas, and without even seeing my gaze he fulfills my silent request.

"What do you mean, not coming?" he asks, his eyebrows raised in surprise. Thank the stars for Thomas. When we were younger, he always played leader to our gang. He was the oldest, and he knew how to reach out, whether to a kid with a scraped knee or to a fence with a NO TRESPASSERS sign.

Or to a boy suggesting the impossible.

Forrester looks around at us, his eyes searching. I don't know what he's looking for, but he doesn't find it. When his face sinks with understanding, my stomach drops in time with the fall of his already frowning mouth.

"I guess you don't know," he says. He lowers his head until his sun-streaked hair obscures his eyes. "I guess you wouldn't."

He chews on his thumbnail and stares at the scratched bench beneath his feet.

"Tell us now," I say, trying for a combination of gentle interest and commanding force. *I'm a bitch, but I still care* — as my charming mother would say. I rub his wide shoulders, the movement my go-to, the way I always comfort my brother and sister.

"My parents got divorced, about four years ago," Forrester replies with a shrug. He might be trying to shrug me away, but I don't let myself be shaken off.

"Seriously?" I ask, glancing behind me. We never established if the twins were as detached from Simon as the rest of us, but Allison and Eli share the same gobsmacked expression as everyone else around this picnic table. At least we're all on the same confused page of this crappy book.

Lots of people get divorced. But Forrester's news is still weird. His parents used to be happy, or at least it seemed like it to me. Sure, Aunt Shirley wasn't quite the lover of the outdoors her husband was. But, shit, my parents spend half their time doing things one of them hates, and it's never strained their relationship.

Of course, I don't actually know a damned thing about Shirley and Simon's matrimony. I haven't seen Forrester's family in ten years. And ten years ago, I didn't care what our parents were up to, so long as it didn't interfere with my fun. Still, the news sits heavily on my lungs. My dad is a Facebook junkie. I know he hasn't talked to his brothers in years. But I find it hard to believe he *never* heard this news through the online grapevine of gossiping grown-ups.

Forrester raises his eyes, but not to look at any of us. He gazes at the playground a ways off in the park. It's full of laughing children, their squeals musical and mocking.

"It was messy, the divorce," he says, the words so quiet they're hard to decipher. I lean in to hear him better and notice his cheeks are sunken. He hasn't eaten much in the last few days, I bet. "I don't really know what happened. They'd been arguing a lot for a while. Then the arguments turned into fights, and then the fights turned into a divorce. Mom married some business guy she met in Toronto six months later. A far cry from me and Dad. He already had two kids of his own, and they're happy now, I guess. She's started over with a whole new family. I think that suits her."

"Forrester," I breathe, but I can't complete the thought. "I'm sorry" lingers behind my lips, stupid and unhelpful. His dad just died. There's no point in me apologizing now for his parents' well-past divorce.

"That's still no excuse for her not to be here," Allison says, her voice tinged with annoyance.

"Wouldn't she want to come — for you, at least?" Kayla adds.

Forrester scoffs, shaking his head.

"She doesn't care about Dad or me. She moved last year. New guy's American, and they're living somewhere in Colorado now." He lets out a long breath. Any glint of anger he may have been stoking is snuffed out by it. "When my parents split, I got a choice, and my choice was to stay with Dad. She made a new life without us in it, and that doesn't change now Dad's ..." he trails off, the words cut short by a breath sharp and scared.

"So, who have you been staying with since ... since Tuesday?" Kayla asks, interrupting my fantasy of hunting Shirley down and giving her a good slap for making her son do something like this on his own. It takes a beat for me to understand her question, but when I do, my fury increases. If Aunt Shirley is out of the picture, and none of us saw him last week, it's not difficult to guess who Forrester has, or has not, been with since the death of his father.

Uncle Simon died at work, and when I heard how it happened I thought it was an awful place to go. Now I'm not so sure. I'm glad he had his heart attack at the construction site and not at home. If he'd been at home, his son would have found him.

Forrester avoids answering the question, which gives us all answer enough. He turned eighteen at the end of May. He's a big boy, capable of spending a few days on his own. Even if by all accounts he shouldn't.

"How does he look?" he asks, veering the conversation to a new morbid topic.

Visitation will be wrapping up soon. The actual burial service will take place graveside, where my uncle will join his parents who died in a car crash before I was born. I'm not going to the service. I'll take my siblings home, where we'll eat junk and dance to music loud with drumming until our parents get back and my mother snaps at us to turn it off. Then I'll choose one of the boys from my contacts list and drown the memories of today in sweat and kisses.

But right now my uncle's still inside the funeral home, lying in his shiny new casket with his eyes closed and his hands folded over his ribs. I didn't study the body or anything, but I saw enough of it when I arrived to know he looked poised and groomed, neat and tidy. And dead. He definitely looked dead.

I don't want Forrester to see it. Remembering his father hours before his death is much better than remembering him days afterwards.

"He looks good," Nolan says, when no one else manages to speak. "They did a good job with everything. It's all ... tasteful."

"Good."

Forrester nods his head and then slumps into silence. I continue rubbing his back, while on the other side of the street the first mourners to leave slide like shadows across the parking lot. Lucky bastards. They'll go home and forget anything sad even happened. I thought I would too, until I got here and remembered Forrester. It's a fitting punishment. I'll feel guilty when I go home to two parents and a couple of siblings. But I *should* feel guilty. Before today, I hadn't given a fucking thought to anything more than the money I'd miss out on by not flipping burgers this afternoon.

Forget Aunt Shirley. I should be giving myself a good slap for being so selfish.

"What will you do now?" Eli asks after a long moment of quiet has passed. I jump, startled by the sudden noise, Eli's voice far deeper than I would have imagined from his gangly figure. I guess I'd been expecting a child's voice. Part of me wants to believe it's still a group of children sitting here.

"What do you mean?" Forrester asks, struggling to focus.

"Well, now that your father's dead and your mother's gone," Eli continues, his heavy voice dropping onto the table like hunks of lead. Eli was always blunt as a child. I don't know whether it's enchanting or a major disappointment to see he's retained the quality.

"Eli," Allison hisses.

She gives her brother a sharp nudge, but Eli's look stays blank. He's unaware he's made any remark someone might consider insensitive.

"I'm not sure," Forrester says, unbothered by Eli's phrasing. "I keep asking myself that question, but I'm really not sure. One thing at a time, I guess. I've given notice on our apartment, and there's an outstanding mortgage on the cottage, so the bank's going to be selling it. I'll be going up there next weekend to get it ready for showing ... some agent called and said they wanted to try their hand at a quick sale to take advantage of the late-season warmth."

"You have to pack up the cottage all by yourself?" I ask.

Forrester shakes his head. "No, there'll be movers for that. I just have to go and clean it up, clear out the personal stuff, that sort of thing. Make it ready for showing, whatever the hell that means."

"But next weekend is Thanksgiving," Kayla says.

My eyes are wide with incredulity. "And you'll be there all alone?"

"No," Thomas says, before Forrester can reply. "No way. You spending the whole weekend up there?"

"Yeah." Forrester nods.

"I'll come up, then," Thomas says. "We'll do it together. Nolan, you can come, too."

Nolan flounders in surprise until he catches his brother's gaze. Then he nods.

"Sure, I'll come up," he agrees.

The relief is easy to see in Forrester's eyes. He probably hadn't even thought to ask for help, but it's obvious he needs it. The task would be momentous under the best of circumstances, cleaning and packing things away to get ready for a sale. But the cottage has been around longer than any of us, and to go there alone, and because of what happened …

"I'll come, too," I blurt. I have to work next weekend, and I've already made plans with friends. But my plans can go to hell. I can't ignore this. Even with Thomas and Nolan there, it'll be hard work going through the entire cottage.

"Thanks, Hailey," Forrester says, and I smile in spite of myself.

"I'll be there as well," Kayla chimes in.

"I can't guarantee I'll be the best company," Forrester says, his lips smirking, his eyes not.

"Count us in, too," Allison says, gesturing to herself and her brother. "I'll have to cash in some favors, but I think I can get next weekend off."

Eli gives his twin a sideways glance he thinks the rest of us don't see. If it were up to him, he'd make an excuse to avoid this excursion. But Allison responds to his look with a pointed stare of her own, and Eli backs down under his sister's glower.

"We'll need the address," he adds, not bothering to disguise his discontent. "I don't think I can get us there by memory."

Nolan's quick to pull his phone from his pocket. He makes a note to himself with the address and inputs our numbers so he can text it to us later.

My parents won't be thrilled when I tell them of our plan. This isn't a group of random kids I met while walking in the park, and it's not like I haven't stayed out way past curfew with boys I barely know, anyway. But they'll have a hard time wrapping their heads around why I want to go.

If they ask, I'll keep it simple and cite the guilt. My mother will roll her eyes, and Dad's face will turn red, but then they'll understand. They have to. No way are they guiltless themselves. They might even suggest coming with me, rallying a few more adults to help get everything in order. I'll fight against them if they do, though. I don't want them there. I don't want any of the parents there. It's their fault we're sitting here as vague acquaintances in the first place.

Spending a weekend with people I haven't seen in years might be fucking awful. We might have nothing in common, and by the time the weekend is over we might still be nothing more than distant relatives.

But if the stars favor us, there's a chance this horrible week could offer at least one happy outcome. The odds might be garbage, but I'm willing to risk it.

Once the details have been confirmed, Kayla stands, stretching her short neck as she watches the figures milling around the funeral home's parking lot.

"I'd better get back," she says with an apologetic shrug.

I nod, giving Forrester's shoulders a final squeeze before I join her.

"Marissa and Liam will be in desperate need of company," I agree. Mom and Dad will stay until the end, but I'll take my sister and brother home soon.

"I think it's nearly over, anyway," Allison says as she, Eli, and Nolan mimic our actions and get up from the table. Thomas is the only one to stay seated with Forrester.

"Want to go get a coffee or something?" he asks.

Forrester shrugs his shoulders again, his expression cloudy like he's unable to make the decision for himself. Thomas catches my gaze, and his head tilts in an almost imperceptible nod. The rest of us are welcome to go, but he won't leave Forrester alone.

"Come on, I'm starved. We'll get some doughnuts, too," he says, half-hauling Forrester up. "I'll even let you have the one with sprinkles," he adds in a tempting voice. I remember those special mornings as kids when fresh doughnuts were brought in for a surprise sugary breakfast. Forrester always wanted something with sprinkles, but with Thomas nearby, he never had the chance.

Now Thomas grins, and after a long, hesitant pause, Forrester smiles in return.

I let all the air out of my lungs, drawing a fresh breath as I link arms with Kayla and head back to the funeral home.

KAYLA

DESPITE THE WARM WEATHER, the signs of fall are around us. Three days after my uncle's funeral, I have to brush a scattering of red-orange leaves from the hammock in my backyard before I climb onto it and dial Hudson's number. I watch the streaking white of a plane flying overhead as I wait for him to answer. Except for the plane, the sky is clear, and looking up, it's easy to imagine I'm staring at a sky made in August. Fall beneath me, summer above. The mingling of the seasons is like living within a new climate altogether.

"Hello, gorgeous," a sly voice says through the speaker.

I smirk, pressing the phone closer to my ear as if it can bridge the over two-hundred-mile gap between Sudbury and Aurora. I still don't understand why Hudson had to go to Laurentian University. There are tons of schools closer to home. Why couldn't he be living in Guelph or Hamilton? Better yet, why couldn't he have gone to York and commuted from our hometown?

"Hey, Hudson," I sigh, heat warming my cheeks after hearing him speak just those two words. I'm pathetic. Hudson's been my boyfriend for more than a year, my friend since elementary school. But whenever he so much as hints at the intimacy between us, I melt.

Still, it's hard to mind being pathetic, when pathetic feels so nice.

"What's up, hun? You never call during the week."

He's correct, but only because of habit. Hudson's parents never let him talk on weeknights when we were both still in high school. Now he's a freshman in university, and I suppose he can talk whenever he wants. But he's only been away for six weeks, and it takes a while to figure out a new routine. Besides, we mostly text or video chat, anyway. Calling him at all is a rarity now, weekday or otherwise.

But this is too important for a text and too urgent to wait for our usual Friday night video chat.

"Look, there's a bit of a problem with this weekend," I tell him. A breeze blows hair across my eyes. I try to clear my line of sight with my free hand.

"Don't tell me your parents decided to have dinner on Saturday," he says. I can hear the muted sounds of his roommate playing a video game. "To the right!" Hudson calls, and something that sounds like gunfire rattles in the background.

"No," I say with enough force to pull his attention back. "We're still having dinner on Sunday."

Hudson's only coming home for two days over the Thanksgiving break. He's driving down Saturday morning, and we're spending the day together before each of our families has Thanksgiving on Sunday. Or, at least, we were. I've been putting off telling him about the change of plans. I haven't seen Hudson since he left for school at the end of August. This weekend is supposed to include one full day of him and me making up for every second we've lost over the past month and a half.

Only, now things have changed.

Gazing out across the backyard, I listen to the wooden wind chimes clattering from their post by the deck as I lower my foot to the ground and give the hammock a push.

"Okay, then, what's up?" he asks.

My breath is quiet as I work to hide my unease. "I'm not going to be around."

Even admitting this much hurts. Six weeks is nothing in terms of habits and learning to break them. But six weeks without the boy I've spent almost every day with over the last year?

My heart burns with the reality of our separation, and the anticipation of seeing him — of holding his hand and hugging and kissing him until my body's so weak I can't stand — has been enough to keep my dreams full and my sleep restless. I didn't think about Hudson when I agreed to go to the cottage this weekend. If I had, perhaps I would have made an excuse to bow out.

I can't quite decide what would have been the better decision. I won't back out now that I've made a promise to help, but my conviction doesn't diminish the awful pinch in my chest. After this weekend, Hudson won't be back until sometime in November. He's not even coming back now for the proper length of the weeklong break he gets from classes. Saturday's the only day we get to see each other, and I'm throwing it away for a group of people I don't even know anymore.

I tell him what's happened. He knows about my uncle, of course. He knew within hours of me knowing myself, and we've talked — or at least texted — every day since then.

"I get that you want to help your cousin," Hudson says once I've related all the details. The background is quiet now, no more firing guns or other pixelated explosions in the distance. Hudson must have crept out into the hallway. "But you haven't seen these people in forever. So why do you have to see them now? I mean, can't you put it off until next weekend? Or, you know, make plans to go out for dinner sometime? Come on, Kayla. It's our one day together."

His frustration makes the ache worse, although I'm not upset enough to shed tears, which is a relief.

"It's important I go," I say, proud to hear the self-righteous gleam creeping into my own words. I cry too often, and I'm impressed my voice is as steady as my cheeks are dry. "I know I haven't seen them in a long time, but ..."

I try to think up the correct response. Claiming family as the be-all-end-all excuse won't do. I share bloodlines with these people, but that doesn't mean we have to be close, that we even have to like each other. And Hudson is family, too. He's not blood, but he's heart, and to me that means more. Still, there was something special about me and my cousins, once. We weren't just relatives. We were friends. And friends are heart, too.

Besides, something else has been nagging at me since Saturday. I keep remembering the way my dad stood watching his brothers at the funeral, all of them present, none of them communicating.

"When you're seven and your parents stop talking to your relatives, you don't think to ask why," I say, hoping Hudson remembers enough of my family's history not to get lost in my rambling. "I'm not sure I even noticed, at least not for a while. And when I did notice, well — time had passed. It's not something you keep track of ... and that's a problem. Hudson, I need to figure out what happened. I want to know why my dad stopped talking to his brothers. They were close once. All of us were. I'm ashamed of myself for never giving it more thought before."

Hudson is quiet on the other end of the line. The silence is not unusual. He's reflective, taking his time to work through his thoughts.

"It does seem odd," he says at last, his voice both disappointed and intrigued, "that your dad would stop talking to his brothers in the first place. I mean, I know your dad ... I never would have guessed he'd be the type to hold that sort of grudge."

"I wouldn't have, either," I say, relieved he understands at least this part of it.

Before, my father had been alone in his estrangement. But now I know the fight goes deeper. None of the siblings, not one in a family of five, have spoken in years. And I have no idea why.

"Have you ever questioned anyone about what happened?" Hudson asks.

I roll my shoulders to keep them from tensing. "No. How could I? What kind of conversation would that be?"

"One in which you find out the murderous secret of the Hacher Slasher," Hudson replies in a dramatic tone.

I'm prepared to argue with him, and it takes a moment for my brain to process what he's just said. Then I laugh.

"The only obvious explanation," I say, my voice as close to deadpan as I'm ever able to make it.

"If you're so interested," Hudson says, his own voice gliding back to its former seriousness, "I'll ask your dad what happened."

"Don't you dare!"

The exclamation is too quick and sharp for my panic to be mistaken. Hudson fits in well with my family, but he doesn't have much self-restraint when it comes to mysteries on his mind. If he gets overly curious about what occurred between my relatives ten years ago, there'll be no stopping him ringing up my dad for an unacceptable chat.

I'm curious about it all myself, if curious is a strong enough word. But firing blunt questions at Dad isn't the way to handle the issue. Besides, if the funeral didn't open him up, my — or my boyfriend's — prying questions won't change anything.

"Fine, I won't ask," Hudson says, defeated. "But, Kayla, are you sure you have to go? I mean, it's our day. Our *one* day together. You're going to give that up to clean a friggin' cottage?"

My stomach tightens, the hard press like someone trying to squeeze my waist into a corset. I tumble out of the hammock and walk across the backyard, trying to ignore the guilty pang his words bring. Our *one* day together. And I'm throwing it away to sweep some floors.

The breeze is cooler now, and it wraps my neck in a shiver of goosebumps. Fall sneaking through summer's stronghold. I wish it were still August, when Hudson was only five minutes away, ready to appear on my doorstep at the slightest hint I wanted him close. When one day didn't mean anything because every day was time we shared.

"I have to go," I say, voice pinched despite my best effort to make the words sound upbeat. "And I know it sucks. And I know it makes me a terrible girlfriend."

"You're not … it's just … damn it, Kayla."

He sounds slumped, like he's dropped to the floor and is sitting with his knees pulled into his chest. I can picture him like that, his sandy hair in need of a cut, an old hoodie on over brand new jeans and sneakers he'll be picking at with his left hand while he grips the phone in his right. I smile, and then sink into the guilt once more.

"I know," I mumble, hoping this isn't messing up something more than one day of seeing each other.

I've had nightmares about our relationship. Horrible dreams I won't tell anyone about because they'll all think it's stupid. Dreams about us drifting apart or being snapped apart by dark forces. I hated Hudson leaving, and I'm still hurt he did. But I never saw him leaving as an end to us, and I don't believe he did, either. People say it all the time, tell me we're idiots for sticking together long-distance while he's off exploring university and I'm at home living the boring life of a high school senior.

I don't care about the what-ifs. Except for the what-ifs of Hudson not being in my life anymore.

But as much as we talk, as much as he smiles over lagging videos or sends me mushy texts throughout each day, I don't have an honest idea of what's going on in Hudson's life now. He's so far away, much further than the physical distance would suggest. I miss him. I want him. I need him with me.

And I'm delaying those things even more by giving up our time together this weekend. Delaying it, or worse — maybe throwing it away altogether.

"Look, I've got to go," Hudson says, his words lengthening as I imagine his body is, too. He's standing, returning to his noisy dorm. I hear the click of the door and the video game sounds resurrected in the background.

"Hudson —"

I don't want this conversation to be over yet. I want to push past this news and end the night on breezy subjects like classes and what's on TV. But he has other plans. We're not in sync, and that terrifies me.

"We'll talk tomorrow, okay?" he says.

This phone call has not lasted nearly long enough. I should say something to keep him on the line. But his tone is definite, and I don't know how to argue against the suggestion of it.

"Yeah, o-okay," I mumble instead, my eyes closing tight as I work to keep the tears at bay.

"Night, Kayla," Hudson says.

"Night, Hudson," I whisper, waiting for the final three words of our conversation, a small token of devotion and normalcy. But they don't come. He hangs up, leaving me on a dead line.

I walk up the steps of the deck and make my way to the back entrance of the house. Light shines out from the kitchen, and when I slide open the door, the smell of roast beef reminds me of the dinner we'll be having in an hour's time. I was looking forward to it before. Now I'm not sure I'll be able to stomach the heavy meat.

Crossing to the counter, I turn on the faucet and fill the kettle so I can make some tea. In the living room, Mom and Dad are watching some home and garden show, and I listen to the overenthusiastic narration of the host as the water hisses and steams. Normally, I would take my tea and join them, admiring the renovation projects and fantasizing about the luxury house I might someday be able to afford. But things have been different since the funeral. Tension has not only coiled around Hudson and me — it's stretched beyond one relationship to also pry apart the easy rapport I've always held with Mom and Dad.

My parents are resistant to the idea of me joining the others at the cottage. Their displeased reaction to my explanation of what occurred last Saturday was unexpected, and when I pressed to know why they didn't agree that helping Forrester would be the best thing to do, Dad grew broody and silent. Even when I turned to Mom, I found no ally. She shrugged her shoulders at my pleading look, offering me nothing but a rigid reminder that my cousins are not the children I used to know.

I assured them my mind was made up, and they haven't protested since. But I suspect their silence comes less from acceptance than from a place of guilt. My parents didn't spare Forrester much consideration in the aftermath of Simon's death. Now his dreary future is weighing on them. But I'm not going to the cottage to ease my conscience, and I wish their lack of objection didn't arise from some fractured hope I'll act as an extension of their own lackluster goodwill.

The kettle boils, drowning the sound of the television. I prepare peppermint tea and grab a box of cookies from the cupboard before sitting at the kitchen table by myself.

The tea warms my hands as I cup the porcelain mug, while the question of why I *am* so determined to take part this weekend continues to bubble like the boiling water from the kettle. At the time, it seemed the only logical choice to offer my assistance at the cottage. Forrester needs help, and we all deserve the chance to figure out what's happened in our lives over the past ten years. Plus, I wanted — want — to see my cousins again. But even as I lift the mug to my lips, I can't shake Mom's terse warning.

My cousins are not the children I used to know.

The tea is bitter as the uncertainty of this statement sinks in. I don't actually know if Mom is right, because I have no idea what these people are like anymore. A couple of years ago, I looked up my cousins online. I remember stalking their profiles and trying to guess at their personalities. But I stayed in stealth mode, never commenting on any posts or following them. To do so felt like an imposition I wasn't prepared to make. After all, it was *my* dad who broke ties with everyone else. At least, I believed so at the time.

After the funeral, armed with a new connection and the surprising discovery that everyone was as isolated from the family as me, I searched for them again. Only this time, I wasn't so successful. Eli and Ali's accounts are all set to private, and what photos I did find tagged with their names are of people I don't know. Nolan is everywhere, but his profiles consist of snippets of video footage: artistic pieces that don't ever showcase him or his brother. I couldn't even locate the other three. Which means they're not online, or — more likely — they're not using their real names.

I am online, though. Instagram, Snapchat, even Tumblr. I'm present and unhidden, my accounts public and created using my real name. So why hasn't anyone followed me?

Hudson doesn't like the idea of this weekend, and neither do my parents. Maybe that means my choice was wrong. Or maybe it just means I'm willing to put the effort into learning the truth about my family. I wish I knew for certain how my jumbled heart truly swayed. If only my cousins weren't such foreign concepts to me now. If only I was sure they were indeed the best friends I used to have.

Hanging on the kitchen's far wall is a familiar picture, a print of a painting we've had as long as I can remember. I take a cookie from the box and study the painted rocks and waters of Georgian Bay as I ruminate over the possibilities and consequences this weekend will bring. A tree juts from pink-gray stone, its limbs and leaves drifting sideways through a gust of wind, while a yellow-clouded sky presides over a wavy shoreline of brown rock and further green trees.

I stare at the artwork, chewing and swallowing as my thoughts slowly return to the afternoon of the funeral. An image of me and my six cousins seated around a picnic table is mentally superimposed over the rough terrain of the painting. My smile is sad as I remember the struggle of that day, the joy of seeing the others and the fight to forget why it was we were finally back together.

Shifting in my seat, the memory clears as I'm startled back into giving my undivided attention to the painting. A sudden shock strikes through me, bringing with it a new curiosity about the way our family used to be and the mystery of why we fell apart.

For the first time in my life, I understand the significance — or at least the irony — of the picture hanging on my kitchen wall. Its title is *Stormy Weather, Georgian Bay*, and it was painted by Frederick H. Varley, one of the original members of the Group of Seven.

ALLISON

Friday, October 7th, 2016
59°F, partly cloudy, 4 MPH winds — NNE

Last night I dreamed I was in a casket. I woke in darkness, and when I opened the casket's lid, I was in the middle of a lake. I knew the lake. I'd been there before. I looked to my left, and there was the cottage. My cousins were standing on the docks next to the water, watching me float. I couldn't see their expressions. I couldn't figure out if they were trying to help me or if they were happy to see me floating away.

Wow. My subconscious is, like, _so_ subtle.

We're going to the cottage tomorrow. I'm supposed to be landscaping the gardens at the museum, but I called in a favor and got the shift switched, so my weekend's clear. Eli doesn't want to go, but he's my ride, so he doesn't have a choice — the ass. I know we haven't seen them in a while, but our cousins _are_ family. And Forrester needs help.

So, we're going. And I don't care if Eli wants to complain the whole weekend or not. It's a long drive and an uncomfortable situation, but at least he gets out of the house for a while. Away from Dad. Which is always a good idea.

I've been watching the weather reports. A storm is on its way. Bad omen, maybe. Or, more likely, a cold front sweeping in to make October feel less like August. The crisp air will be a relief from the stuffy heat. An early dusting of snow would be brilliant, too, though I doubt the temperature drop will be quite so severe.

Maybe this weekend is a mistake. Storm or no, the forecast is cloudy, even if I can't pinpoint why I'm so certain the clouds will be covering _us_.

At least I'm making the effort. For Forrester's sake. And for Dad's — for the days when he was the family historian, sitting us in his study and showing us old photographs of people long dead. Back in the golden time when he readily declared that family is the root of everything.

Those days are gone now, and his sentiments have rotted into bullshit. But I'm curious to see if there was ever any truth to it. Curious, and a bit terrified.

I don't know what's happened to make me afraid of spending two days with the people I used to call my friends.

NOLAN

"NOLAN, ARE YOU GOING to text the entire drive up to the cottage?"

My brother gives me an annoyed half-glance as he snaps his seatbelt into place and switches on the car's ignition.

"If I watch you drive, I might have an anxiety attack," I mutter. He punches my arm and adjusts the rear-view mirror. "Ow!" I rub the spot, a laugh breaking through the groan. Thomas grins, putting the car in reverse and pulling out of the driveway.

This afternoon the black interior of the car will be sticky and hot, but this early in the morning an unmistakable fall chill breezes through the sky. Thomas hates it. He already misses summer, when 6:00 a.m. is warm enough to keep the sunroof open and the seats of his Volkswagen GTI always smell like the beach. I'm not so attached to the season, although I do miss not having the weekly obligation of school.

Still, Thomas is happy this morning. He's missed the cottage. I don't remember much about it. Despite Thomas's belief that the place is so freaking amazing it should be a permanent fixture in my memory, I was only six the last time we went there. Anyway, I'm sure Thomas remembers enough for both of us.

"Summer was glorious on the bay," he told me last night as we packed our weekend bags. "And no matter the time of year, it was a haven away from the incessant noise of the world."

He grinned, and then the grin faded into a sadder moment of recollection.

"Bad things didn't happen at the cottage," he admitted. "I never imagined I could go there for a reason like this, to pack it up because my uncle's dead and my cousin has no parents … or home."

Now, Thomas presses the gas and rushes through a yellow light before making a hard turn into the Tim Hortons parking lot.

"What the hell, Thomas? Let's try to make it to the cottage in one piece, okay?" I say, gripping the passenger door. I can't wait until I get my full driver's license. I'm not letting my reckless brother drive me anywhere once I've graduated from my pointless G1.

Thomas swerves quickly into the drive-thru to bug me, and I let out a long breath, hunching into my seat to read an incoming message on my phone.

> B: Morning, babe. Are you alone?
> Something crazy happened last night.
> We need to talk.

I stare at the screen in surprise, angling it toward the door so Thomas won't be able to glimpse the latest text.

> Me: In the car with Thomas on
> our way to the cottage.
> Can't talk, but can text.
> What's up?

> B: Shit, was hoping I'd get you before
> you left. Okay, text it is. You ready?
> Because I certainly wasn't.

> Me: I'm all eyes. Text away.

"What do you want?" Thomas asks, dropping some trash into the bin as he pulls forward and waits for the voice over the speaker to give him the go-ahead to order.

"What?" I blink in surprise, turning off the screen as I realize what he's asking me. "Oh. Coffee, please. Double-double."

Thomas relates my order to the metal box, getting himself the same thing plus a pack of Timbits. Mom insisted we bring a box of Danishes she bought from the bakery with us, but neither one of us can wait three hours to eat anything. Thomas likes ordering food while he's driving, anyway. In his mind, trips worthy of provisions are always the best.

When we pull up to the window, Thomas flirts with the drive-thru attendant while I check my phone. No message has come through yet, which means this text is going to be a long one.

My knee is bouncing, and I force it to stop so Thomas won't catch on to the telltale sign of my nerves. Not that it matters. When he's paid for our order and has finished his obnoxious flirtation with the shy girl I'm pretty sure is terrified of his hungry eyes, he hands me my coffee and glances at the phone clutched too-tight in my fist.

"What's Brandon up to this weekend?" he asks as we peel away from the window.

The question is casual but nevertheless prying, and I slide the phone under my leg so I can open the lid of my drink.

"Hanging out with Bea, I think," I say as we turn back onto the road. "She's back in town for the holiday."

Thomas quirks an eyebrow, but I pretend not to notice. The fact that my brother spent the summer messing around with my boyfriend's sister is still weird, and her moving out of town last month to live with some guy she liked better than Thomas was a relief for Brandon and me. But as much as Thomas plays it off like his trysts with Bea were nothing more than two buddies reaping the full benefits of their friendship, I know her sudden departure is a sore spot for him.

The phone buzzes, but I grip my coffee tight to stop from checking it right away.

"By the way, you have weird taste in women," I say instead, changing the course of the conversation.

"Lauren has her charms," Thomas says, referring to the drive-thru girl.

He switches lanes and turns onto the highway ramp as I open my coffee and take an initial, cautious sip. I try not to cringe at the bitter taste I'm not sure I'll ever be quite used to. A hot chocolate would have been a nicer beverage, but I started pretending to like coffee six months ago, and I don't have any intention of stopping the charade now — even if everyone important is well aware I don't like the stuff.

"That's not what I mean," I say, licking my lips and thinking I should at least up the sugar count next time I order. "You make no sense. The girls you like. They're so different. That girl back there. She's the total opposite of Asha."

"Yeah, you're right." Thomas smirks.

He focuses on merging onto Highway 400, and I take the moment to pull out my phone and check the message. My eyes grow steadily wider as I read through the lines of carefully typed text. But when Thomas sighs, I shut off the screen and shove it back under my leg.

"I'm greedy. I want them all," he tells me as he flicks the signal so we can change lanes.

I take another disgusting sip of coffee before I'm composed enough to answer with a shake of my head.

"At least you don't discriminate."

Thomas makes quick work of moving to the highway's fast lane. The air outside is cool, but not so cold he doesn't still have the windows halfway down. The wind rushes against us, a great excuse for him not to bother with the radio. He hates listening to music when he drives. Lucky for him, I find a soundtrack in the thumping of the tires and the flapping of the wind.

I drink my coffee and wait for Thomas to get lost in his driving. He's happy to be silent, and it only takes a moment before I'm safe to pull out my phone and spend more time reading the message and crafting a response. The news Brandon has related is shocking, but not definite. And since I can't do anything about it, once I've sent off my reply I stop myself from obsessing over it by digging my camera out of the bag by my feet.

Recording the car's progress as we drive offers me a good distraction, and the video will make decent stock footage for some future movie project. The highway is busy, early morning commuters trying to beat the rush north for their last cottage country weekend of the year. I'd prefer the roads to be a tad emptier for the shot, but I can't blame the other motorists. After all, we're heading up to a cottage as well.

The trip is quiet, small talk interspersed with long stretches of nothing but the noise of the road. I think about Brandon and his message before I ponder what's waiting for us at the end of this lengthy trip. The swirl of thoughts is like white noise of a different kind, comfortable companions to keep me occupied until we reach the highway's exit and head in through Parry Sound.

The slower pace of in-town driving brings Thomas out of his own quiet thoughts. He taps his fingers against the steering wheel until his lack of rhythm irritates me enough that I can't keep silent.

"Will you stop that?" I huff, exasperated.

Thomas smiles as he brings his fingers to a rest.

"Did I tell you I quit?" he says, the words out in a nervous rush.

Thomas is three years older and a great deal more experienced than I am, but I won't deny loving how anxious he gets when making confessions to me. The only downside is that if he's nervous to tell me something, it means he's going to share information I don't want to hear.

"You what?" I bark at him, annoyed he's proven my point. "Thomas, you've got to be kidding me. That's, what, your fifth job this year?"

He shrugs, flexing his fingers against the steering wheel.

"It was working the counter at a gas station. Not what I'd call a dream job."

"At least it was something," I say. "Why'd you quit this time? I thought you didn't mind your boss."

"I didn't," he says as we pull to a stop at a red light. "But I've, uh, I've decided to take off for a while."

A sharp pain, like trying to swallow a chip that hasn't been chewed enough, flares in my stomach.

"Take off where?" I ask, my voice as steady as I can make it.

This kind of declaration is not unheard of from him. A weekend with a new girlfriend, a nip down to the States for a concert — once it was a three-week camping trip in Algonquin with a rotating cast of friends. But I never like it. Even when he texts me updates whenever he's got a decent signal, Thomas's absences remind me of the week he didn't communicate. If he planned vacations like a normal freaking person, I wouldn't care so much. But Thomas takes off on a whim. I think he likes to pretend he's a leaf, only barely a part of a rooted life and always ready to go wherever a strong wind might send him.

"Out of town. A road trip, maybe?" he says, trying to sound over-casual, as if he's contemplating nothing more than a trek to the mall. "I was thinking out west, to see what else the Great White North has to offer."

I study him with skeptical eyes while he focuses on the road, looking only so far over as to catch me in his peripheral vision.

"You're going to travel the country. By yourself?" I ask. He nods, and with matching fluidity I shake my head. "Why?"

"Why not?" He smiles, trying to pretend this is all normal, like a production crew striking a set and moving to a new locale to prepare for the next shot. "I'm done school, I'm unattached, and I've got no decent job prospects. I can work at a gas station anywhere, if I need money."

I scoff. "Yeah, and how is traveling going to change any of those things?"

"Maybe it won't," he says. His face wears the stupid, blissful expression he once told me he always gets when he reflects on the pure joy of aimless wandering. "But I want to see if it might."

We leave Parry Sound's main roads, a spark of excitement igniting in my brother's face. We're getting close to the cottage now, and he's infinitely more excited about it than I am.

"You're really going?" I ask as we brake at one of the last lights between us and Georgian Bay.

Thomas nods, giving me a steady look before staring back at the road.

"Why not?" he repeats, shifting gears as we pick up speed through the green light. "I was going to leave a couple of weeks ago, but then Uncle Simon died. I'm glad I didn't take off before I heard the news … I'd feel like shit if I ever found out what Forrester was doing up here on his own. All things considered, the timing worked out well. You know, in a twisted sort of way. I think this weekend will be the perfect send-off."

I pick up my phone as it buzzes with a new text. Brandon's message is an instant reminder of why my brother and I are so different, of why I'll never see things like he does. Aimless wandering is a void of meaningless inconvenience to me. Everything I need radiates from home base, and I like it that way. The wind could never lead me on some magical, unplanned journey. If anything, I'm a branch on Thomas's tree, solidly stuck to the trunk with twigs inadequate to keep his leaf close.

My fingers click quickly against the screen of my phone, my mouth set in a line as I try to ignore what my brother has said, all while working to figure out how I will respond. I'm unable to properly voice my frustrations over his flightiness, and I can't show him Brandon's message as a means to explain why this weekend is, in fact, a horrible time for him to duck away from his life. So, after a minute passes in silence, I instead allow my lips to twitch in a small grin.

"What are you going to do about all your girls?" I ask.

Thomas laughs.

"That's the extraordinary thing about girls, my dear brother," he says, grinning as we turn onto a dirt road, an odd familiarity making me realize the cottage can't be far away. "They're everywhere."

KAYLA

LIFTING UP MY SUNGLASSES, I watch as Dad reverses his silver SUV before swinging the car in a three-point turn. The entire drive up here was a tumbling dance of tense silence twirling with sharp reminders he'll pick me up tomorrow at noon. When we got close to the cottage, I had to pull out an actual map, the pain of trying to get a steady signal making it not worth the wasted usage costs of navigating with my phone's GPS. I figured Dad would remember the way, but he said it'd been too long. Liar. He was too preoccupied with being angry, a facade that only fades now as his eyes cast wistfully about the property before his brows furrow and he spares me a final, worried look as he drives down the dirt path back to the main road.

When Dad is out of sight, I haul my duffel bag and purse over one shoulder and head toward the cottage. The wide wooden structure sits atop a small slope, large windows reflecting the nearest trees at its front. Behind it, an open space with a large fire pit is nearest to the back porch, while further away and to the right is an old shed. Straight back and down beyond the fire pit the ground slopes more, until it meets a set of docks that stretch over the calm, shining waters of Georgian Bay.

The day is bright, and the fire pit is lit, the smell of smoke wonderfully thick in the air. But no one is here. Whoever has already arrived could be inside, the cleaning and packing already underway. The thought sends a loose twist of panic springing through me. It's not even ten o'clock yet. I hope I'm not late.

A red car I doubt belongs to Forrester is parked near the cottage's front entrance. I don't know much about cars, but the sleek, sporty design suggests this one is too expensive for any teenager to be driving. I don't think Uncle Simon was rich, and I can't imagine Forrester would want to drive something so flashy on dirt and gravel roads. When I spot the beat-up Jeep parked down the slope by the shed, I smile. The muck-green color reminds me of the Jeep Uncle Simon used to drive in the summers of my childhood. I squint, wondering if it could be the same vehicle.

"Kayla!"

The Jeep is forgotten as I spin around, the sound of a distant voice directing my attention back to the fire. Allison waves to me, a pile of wood held against her chest. I walk up the wide-planked stairs of the cottage's back porch to drop my bags before joining her.

As I approach the pit, Allison adds another log to the stone-rimmed circle. Folding camp chairs have been placed around the fire, and I sit while Allison stokes the small flames. Her beige sweater and brown corduroys are covered in dirt from carrying the wood, but she doesn't seem to care. She gives her front a quick brush with her long, bony fingers as she sits across the circle from me.

"Where's Eli?" I ask, looking around for Allison's twin. They could have come up separately, but it seems like a massive waste of gas if they did.

"With Forrester. They'll be back in a minute," Allison says, picking dirt from the underside of her unpolished nails. The expert way she flicks at the grime is entrancing, but when she raises a hand to her lips and uses her teeth to scrape out a stuck piece, I cringe and stare down at the fire.

We sit in silence, Allison oblivious to my disdain, until I hear a low murmuring off to my right. Two figures walk toward the house, each carrying an armload of firewood. Before them, a mud-splotched dog leads the way in a sprint, and when it notices a new arrival, it sets its sights on me. Tail wagging, it bounds to where I sit, two big, muddy paws landing in my lap as it welcomes me with a happy bark.

"Runner, get down, boy!" Forrester calls, and the dog's head twitches to one side before he obeys the command. He sits down in front of my chair, his tail wagging against the ground.

"Hi, Runner." I smile, petting the dog's head.

I don't have any pets, but I've always wanted a dog. I wipe the mud from my jeans with my free hand, while Runner nuzzles under the press of my other palm. He has the pointed ears and general look of a German shepherd, with the longer, softer fur of some other breed.

"Good boy," Forrester murmurs as he passes. He drops his load of firewood and then gives Runner a pat. "Sorry about that, Kayla," he says, his expression sympathetic and amused.

He looks better today than he did at the funeral. His complexion has lost its haggard paleness, and I can even see a twinge of pink in his cheeks.

"It's fine," I assure him, as Runner paws at me, annoyed my attention's shifted away. I gaze back at the dog and pet him with both hands.

"Hungry?" Forrester asks.

He grabs a heavy skillet from beside one of the camp chairs. When he opens the small cooler beneath it, I glimpse a pack of butcher-quality bacon resting inside. My stomach growls, and I laugh.

"Well, I had a muffin earlier, but ... I could eat again."

"Thought we could have a late breakfast out here before we head inside," Forrester says, before his voice drops and his eyes fix on the skillet in his grip. "I didn't want to go in yet."

I cast a quick glance at the twins, relieved when Eli wipes his hands on his jeans with a sigh.

"Hurry it up, will you? I'm starved," he says.

Forrester lets out a chuckling breath as he sets the skillet overtop the flames. Soon, the bacon spits grease and the eggs sizzle, and I revel in the delicious scents mingling with the smoky fire. We pass plates and cutlery between us, and Thomas and Nolan arrive as the bacon reaches its perfect crispness.

"Ah, great. I'm hungry enough to eat the whole pig!" Thomas declares as he inhales the smell of breakfast and passes around a box of Danishes to accompany the feast.

"That's not an exaggeration," Nolan says, giving us a quick wave of greeting before he slumps into a chair. "If you're not careful, he'll devour the entire pack of bacon while your back is turned."

His fingers move quickly over the keyboard on his phone, even as he speaks. He must be texting someone. I'm surprised his signal strength is so good. When I checked my own phone before Dad and I arrived, I only had one bar of reception.

Forrester serves breakfast, and I eat way more than I should, the meal too good to pass up. By the time the entire packet of bacon has been consumed — Thomas managing to wolf down a good third of it himself — my stomach is swollen as I lean back in my chair, full and satisfied.

Hailey's car pulls into the drive as we're finishing up the meal. I hear it before I see it, the stereo loud with music incomprehensible from this distance. Lyrics about truth and myth sung by a low female voice are all I can make out, the words and notes ones I don't recognize.

"Hope I'm not late!" Hailey calls from the open window.

She switches off the engine, and the sudden absence of her stereo is as thunderous as the pulsing bass had been.

"You missed breakfast!" Thomas yells over his shoulder as he swipes his last piece of bacon through the remnants of maple syrup sticking to his plate.

"Ate already," Hailey replies with a smile. She slides out of the yellow car, patting the dent over the left headlight as she walks around to the passenger-side door. "I brought someone with me," she adds as she reaches for the handle.

I glance at the others, uneasy to hear Hailey's arrived with company. The official purpose of this weekend is to clean the cottage, but I had my heart set on spending this time with my cousins — *only* my cousins.

I twist my neck to see who her companion is, pinching annoyance giving way to embarrassed relief when Hailey opens the door and a collie jumps out of the car. Runner's ears perk up and he barks, his tail creating a miniature cloud of dirt as it thumps against the ground. He resists temptation for about ten seconds before he runs for the collie, and soon both dogs are sniffing each other, bouncing in careful circles until they determine whether they can be friends.

"I didn't know you had a dog," Forrester says, smiling.

Hailey approaches us, rose-tinted sunglasses covering half of her face. Her long black hair is twisted into a braid slung across her shoulder, and she wears a cream-colored sweater and a pair of faded blue jean shorts. Hanging down over her chest is a necklace: a leather strap with two wooden beads and a long white-gray feather dangling at the bottom. She strokes the feather as she joins us by the fire, a wide grin on her face.

"Had her for six years now," she says, relating the story of how she came to own her pet. "Found her by the side of the road when she was a puppy. We tried to find her owners, but no one ever claimed her. She's been ours for a long time now, though."

"What's her name?" Nolan asks, clutching his phone against his leg like he's waiting to feel it buzz.

"Star," Hailey says, and then she laughs. "Actually, it's Starburst. Named her after my favorite candy. But we call her Star."

"Looks like her and Runner made out okay," Forrester says.

He motions toward the two dogs running in circles, each taking turns to chase the other. For a moment the canines attract all of our attention. Then Hailey takes a few steps closer to the fire, her hands on her hips and her head cocked to one side.

"We've got two days to clean this place up, and we're all sitting outside ... why?"

I look down at my feet, studying the chipped pink polish on my toes like it's a fascinating work of art. But to my surprise, the question doesn't hang tense and unanswered. Instead, it's Forrester himself who replies.

"Well," he begins. I glance back up to see him surveying the group of us. His eyes move from one person to the next, and for a brief moment our gazes catch. Then he looks at Hailey, offering her a somewhat hesitant smile. "We were waiting for you."

Hailey's lips soften as she walks over to Forrester and grabs his arm, hauling him up as Eli and Allison put out the fire. Nolan makes another check of his phone, and Thomas and I call after the dogs, who run to join us on the path up to the cottage's back porch.

HAILEY

FORRESTER SLIDES THE KEY into the lock, turning it halfway before his hand stills.

"Sorry if the air's a bit stale," he says, his fingers jerking the lock the rest of the way. He twists the knob and pushes the back door open. "We haven't been here in a few weeks. We were supposed to come up last weekend, but ..." He stops again, his knuckles pressed white against his keys.

I guess I should be concerned about the way his sentence remains unfinished, but try as I might, I can't get my eyes to stop staring at his skin. Squeezed so tight, his fingers are *literally* white. Pure white. As opposed to his usual tone, which is more tanned — but still white.

So many shades of the same damn color. We should have better names for these things. Forrester is a sun-boy, golden brown and toasty. And then there's someone like Allison, her skin pink, half with zits and half from natural blush. But they're still white. And the best part is, my skin is a mere notch darker than Forrester's, but he is white, and I am not.

Shit. Looks like I've now become the kind of person who refers to others as *white kids*.

Last week I didn't notice my cousins' varying complexions. But now the lightness of their skin shines like a constellation of my past. I spent my whole life believing I was the same as them, but as soon as I saw everyone crowded around the fire this morning, the difference between my being and theirs struck hard. If I'd come here a year ago,

I wouldn't have paid any heed to Forrester's fingers, except to examine his tight-fisted grip. Ten months can change a life, I guess. In January I fought with my mother, and now here I am in October, identifying myself as a Cree girl and forgetting all about my half-Caucasian blood.

Guilt pools beneath my pores, but I'm not sure why. Perhaps it's because I'm acting like these people aren't my family, when I used to love them more than my own siblings. Or perhaps it's because I made a conscious effort to ignore our differences when we were children, and now I have the hindsight to realize I did so at the expense of my own identity.

Or perhaps it's because Forrester is standing beside me remembering his dad, and I'm being a bitch obsessing about the color of his hand.

"Wow, this place hasn't changed a bit," Thomas says, stepping across the threshold and saving the moment. Thank the stars *twice* for Thomas. At least he's able to think about someone other than himself.

"It's pretty much the exact same," I agree.

The words are out of my mouth before I walk into the main room and look around to discover they are true. The inside of the cottage hasn't changed. Like, at all. The expansive main floor has the same layout, most of the space an open rectangle with a sunken square designated as the living room. Within the square, the same blue flower-patterned couch and brown recliner chair are positioned around the same ornate coffee table.

Fucking hell. Ten years, and not even the position of the furniture has been altered.

"Seriously, ever heard of redecorating?" Thomas teases, grinning as he explores the main floor.

The high wood-slat ceilings reach up past the upper balcony, two windows in the slanted roof letting in streams of bright sunlight. The one thing memory does injustice to is the size of this place.

My experience has been that you tend to remember things huge, only to grow up and find them tiny. But I remembered this place cozy, and turns out it's massive — not even small enough to be a true cottage.

Nope. This sucker's a house, and damn, Forrester's going to get a pretty penny once this goes up for sale. Too bad he'll never be able to afford it again. The value of this place has got to be ten times what it was bought for back in ... whenever the hell it was bought.

"It's perfect, just what a good cottage should be," Kayla says, defending the old charm of this place. She's right, and we all know it — even Thomas.

I walk past the living room and make it across to the adjoining kitchen, the green countertops and light oak cabinets so familiar they make me remember bowls of cereal eaten at the round oak table, our parents moaning about their need for the coffee brewing in the ancient, stained pot.

I was excited to come back here, but I didn't expect to be barraged with mundane memories that are still somehow stupidly charming. As a kid, I never cared much about this place. Growing up, I believed camping was for people too poor to afford a hotel, a conviction I held thanks to the incessant complaints of my mother as we drove up here on early summer mornings. Because, indoor plumbing and hot showers aside, this cottage always felt like one step away from camping. I hated the muddy floors, the wet towels and dripping bathing suits hanging out to dry in the sun. But it looks like I can't help remembering even those irksome traits with fondness now.

I turn back to face the living room again. Thomas is halfway up the stairs, and Nolan's thrown himself onto the couch. The dogs continue their play despite the more constrained space, and Forrester watches them, momentarily distracted by their antics. Eli stands by the back windows looking out over the bay, and Allison walks in circles, staring up at the windows in the ceiling. Kayla's watching the others, like I am. Our eyes meet across the room as she raises her black-framed sunglasses, placing them on her head like a headband.

"Okay, first things first," I say, shifting my gaze back to Nolan. "Rule for the next two days is no phones."

"What?" Nolan's head snaps up, and I quirk a brow, daring him to argue with my declaration.

He's in constant conversation with either a dozen interesting people or a single spectacular one. I wouldn't be surprised to find out Nolan had a girlfriend. He's cute, with his unruly hair, clear blue-green eyes, and full lips. He's about six feet tall, and he's skinny, which makes him appear even taller. Plus, going by the look he's now giving me, I'd say he's got "broody-but-sweet" down pat. He's a fine catch, looks-wise. I'd vouch for his personality, too, if I could. But I don't know him well enough anymore. When he was five or six, he used to be a hellish little brat, collecting bugs and sneaking them into our sleeping bags when we weren't looking. He had an especial love of terrorizing Allison, who nearly fainted whenever an insect came too close.

I hope his manners have improved.

"We came here to help Forrester," I remind him.

"Give it up, Nolan," Thomas says, swooping down the stairs and into the sunken portion of the living room to snatch the phone from Nolan's hand. "Hailey's right. A bit of sun, the bay, and the exciting prospect of cleaning an entire cottage. Who could ask for more? We don't need you staring at your phone all weekend."

Thomas gives his brother a knowing look, and Nolan glares in return.

"Let me say goodbye," he mumbles, reaching for the phone again.

"Oh, I can do that for you," Thomas replies.

Nolan stands, and even though his body is the same height as his brother's, he seems in that moment a few imposing inches taller.

"Don't," he says in a fierce, panicked voice.

I'm about ready to burst out laughing. A new girlfriend, or maybe just a crush. I remember being overprotective of my phone with my first boyfriend or two, when Marissa threatened to send embarrassing, inappropriate texts the moment I left it unguarded. I can see the same tension between Thomas and Nolan now, and for once my sympathies side with the younger sibling.

All my goodwill dissipates when I glance back at Kayla, though. Across the room, her flawless, made-up face now sports a worried expression as she stares at the screen of her own phone.

"Oh, give me a break," I groan. One cousin obsessed with his phone I can handle. But for some reason, two pisses me off. "Don't tell me we're all incapable of going twenty-four fucking hours without being online?"

"What?" Kayla startles, her cheeks flushing with embarrassment. She stares up at me, her eyes guilty like she's just been caught doing something indiscreet. "N-no, I was just making sure —"

"Geez, Hailey, let the girl look at her phone," Allison mutters, interrupting Kayla's stuttering explanation.

I roll my eyes, clenching my jaw to keep from a further outburst as Kayla sneaks a final look at her screen. When she finally shoves the device into the front pocket of her overnight bag, I let my facial muscles relax.

"It's not a problem," she says, her glossy lips pursed with concern. "I was just hoping Hudson would — but never mind. It's fine."

"Good," I say, smoothing my voice into a gentler tone. I'm curious to know who Hudson is, but Kayla drops her eyes, her fingers nervously sweeping back strands of honeyed hair like she's afraid to draw any more attention. I didn't think my remark would make her so flustered. She's like a chastised puppy — I've seen the same wounded look in Star's eyes after we catch her going through the trash, when she tries to worm her way out of punishment by showing us just how damn cute she can be.

I weigh the pros and cons of apologizing for making my cousin so uncomfortable. But with the momentary drama of Kayla's phone over, Nolan distracts everyone by resuming the fight for his own device.

"Thomas," he pleads.

While the brothers continue their standoff, the rest of us fish out our phones and hand them to Kayla to add to her bag.

"Oh, fine," Thomas sighs at last.

He hands back the phone, and relief floods Nolan's face as his fingers glide over the keypad, his message compiled and sent off in a matter of seconds. Then he locks his phone and passes it to Kayla before slinking back to the couch.

"Now that's settled," Thomas continues, giving his brother a warning gaze, "where should we start the cleanup? Docks, woods ..."

"I was thinking the rooms upstairs," Forrester says, running a shaky hand through his brown-blond hair. "There are four rooms. I'll take my dad's, and you can split up the rest."

"Are you sure that's a good idea?" I ask.

Forrester waves away my concern. "Yeah. I ... I need to do this, and I don't want anyone else going through his things, you know?"

"That's fair," Eli says, glancing toward the upper balcony. He sounds bored. He obviously didn't want to come this weekend, and he's doing fuck all to hide his displeasure. If it weren't for Allison, I doubt he'd spare us a thought as he lounged at home or did whatever the hell it is he does in his normal life. "Let's get started."

Unlike the kitchen and the worn living room furnishings, the cottage's upper floor doesn't make me a nostalgic sap. As a kid, I rarely went up this far. Everything I needed was contained within the lower levels. I slept, played board games, or watched movies in the basement rec room. I bathed in the basement bathroom, ate in the kitchen, and spent the rest of the time outside. The upstairs was for the parents. I only ventured up if I needed to find my mother or my dad, and even then I would only ascend after one of my aunts told me to stop yelling for them from the bottom of the staircase.

Now, we go upstairs together and thin out as we pick our rooms. I end up with Allison in one of the guest rooms, which has clearly not been used as a guest room for a long time.

"Look at this place," Allison says, gathering her blond hair into a ponytail before she gets to work. "It's like a massive junk pile."

She ain't kidding. I approach the bed — now acting as a giant shelf for dozens of small boxes, uneven stacks of papers, pieces of clothing, and other assorted bits of crap — and wonder what the hell I've gotten myself into. Tidying knick-knacks and doing a bit of dusting and sweeping was a given for this weekend. But I wasn't expecting a mess like this, and it's obvious Allison wasn't, either. I can't fathom what Forrester would have done if he'd come up here by himself.

"Where should we start?" I ask, surveying the clutter.

"Let's begin with the boxes," Allison suggests, motioning not toward the boxes on the bed but to a stack of boxes pushed against one corner of the wall. "We can organize them, empty some of them, and use the empty ones for other stuff later."

"Whatever you say."

I give her a salute, and then stare at the disaster awaiting me. I hate organizing. But I can see Allison's reasoning. Aside from throwing everything into the trash — which doesn't seem like a *bad* option — there's no other way to conquer this mess.

We start by pulling box after box down from the stack. None of the boxes are sealed, which makes it easy to open the flaps and see what's inside. Most of what we find is work-related, old receipts and invoices for the construction company our uncle operated. Some of these are recent, so we keep them, shuffling the papers until they resemble something like a neat stack before sticking them back into one of the boxes. But some of the papers are old — like, decades old.

"I think we can toss these," Allison says, her button nose crinkled as she tries to read the faded scrawl of one slip. "Some of them aren't even legible anymore."

"I didn't realize Simon was like this," I say, looking at a hand-written invoice from 1995. "I guess I never thought about him as a businessman much."

"Neither did I," Allison agrees. "Do you remember the Christmas we spent here? Our van almost didn't make it through the snow. We got stuck down off the main road, and Uncle Simon, Uncle Jake, and your dad had to help dig us out. That's how I remember him. Digging snow out from under our tires and laughing while my dad cursed a blue streak."

"I remember my mother freaking out because she thought we were playing too close to the water that year." I smirk. She probably had good reason for it, even if we did think she was a raven-haired witch at the time. We complained that she was ruining our fun, and then we spent the remainder of the night building a giant snowman off the back porch instead.

Like the memories of cereal bowls down in the kitchen, new recollections now bob to the surface. I can picture Kayla planning the snowman's face while the rest of us rolled the body, Forrester refusing to wear gloves because he thought they hindered his ability to pack snow. Dirt and sand have never been interests of mine, but snow and ice are another story. Christmas at this cottage is where the stars shine in my memory.

"And I remember drinking hot chocolate while our dads dragged in a giant tree they'd cut from the forest," I add with a grin.

"We decorated it with popcorn and cranberries," Allison says, nodding. "Because we didn't have any actual decorations. Kayla's mom told us it was more authentic that way, but Thomas kept whining because he'd left his favorite decoration on the tree at home."

"Batman, wasn't it?" I ask.

"I think so." Allison laughs. "He was obsessed with Batman."

We both smile until the glimmering recollections dissolve into the piles of junk around us. I pick up another old receipt and stare at my dead uncle's signature near the bottom.

"Like I said, that's how I remember him," Allison mumbles. "Not like this — nothing like this."

"Do you know anything about why they stopped talking?" I ask.

Allison doesn't respond. When I glance up at her, she's shaking her head.

"No. I didn't even know it was everyone. I never stopped to think about it, really."

"Me neither," I admit. "But it's not just some fucked-up nostalgia trip, is it? We were close back then. I remember the whole family being close."

"You're not imagining it," Allison says. She goes back to sorting through papers. "At least, I don't think you are. But obviously something happened. I asked my dad about it, after the funeral. He didn't say much."

"Mine told me there was a fight, but that's pretty much it."

"That's what Dad told Eli and me, too," Allison scoffs. "Kind of a no-brainer. But he wouldn't tell us about *what*. He and Eli got into it, they're so similar, so stubborn."

She pauses like she's on the verge of saying more, but then she stops, focusing on her handful of papers instead.

I'm curious about her tense expression, but I'm not yet ready to pry. If I were in this room with Kayla, or Thomas, or even Nolan or Forrester, I wouldn't hesitate shoving myself into their personal thoughts. I'm not shy, and I firmly believe if people want something to remain hidden they shouldn't go around being so damn obvious they're keeping a secret. But as little as I know any of the people in this cottage, the twins are the only ones to feel like actual strangers.

And out of the two of them, Eli was always more blunt and imposing, so even he has an edge over his sister.

To think I've let someone so close fade so far. Allison didn't make much of a lasting impression on my memory, I guess. She was around as much as everybody else, but of all my cousins, she's the one I've always thought of the least. I'm used to being called a bitch. But I never suspected my selfish tendencies extended all the way back to childhood.

"You think anyone else knows anything?" I ask, shoving those revelations away for another time.

Allison doesn't answer my question. So we continue sorting in silence, the sounds of ruffled papers our main source of company.

"Hey, everyone," Kayla calls some time later, her voice echoing out from one of the other rooms. The sound makes me jump, and I roll my eyes at my skittish nerves. "Come and look at this."

I glance at Allison. She shrugs, and I follow suit before dropping my current handful of receipts and walking out of the room.

THOMAS

I REMEMBER THE LAST time Nolan and I were here.

Summer.

Sun hot, blue-gray blister-hazy sky, mosquitoes swarming on a feast of supple skin.

Nolan bit so bad he had to stay inside, Mom laughing and Shirley bickering, convinced he would die of West Nile before nightfall.

Forrester in the shed, climbing over rusted nails and splintered wood to find the water guns buried under a year's worth of clutter.

Dad and Simon resting in wingbacks on the dock.

Me taking refuge from the bites underneath, floating hidden in the skinny-child space of breath between the waterlogged wood and the moss-glistened bay — listening to the conversation above my head.

Words half mumbled, as my father and his brother talk about a girl.

KAYLA

"WOW, WHERE DID ALL these photos come from?"

Allison grabs half a dozen photos from the bin I've carried downstairs to the living room's coffee table. I drop the lid onto the floor and pull out a few photos myself.

"Time," I say.

I study the selection of photos in my grasp. The pictures vary in age — some are recent, only five or six years old, while others date back to the seventies and even earlier.

Looking at old pictures and seeing the past laid out before my eyes is one of the happiest ways I can think of to dwindle away hours. I plan to study history in university next year, getting my degree in education so I can teach the subject afterwards. Ancient civilizations, wartime stories, diseases, architecture, technology — I'm not picky about the where or when. I simply think there's something fascinating about peering into the lives of generations gone by.

And yet, I know little about the past of my own family. Years ago, I remember visiting the twins and admiring Uncle Joey's mass of family records, listening with rapt attention to his stories about people I didn't know while Allison and Eli groaned and pinched each other to keep themselves entertained. I wanted to take in all he had to offer, but I can no longer recall any of the details of his stories — just as I fail to identify any of the smiling faces in the pictures I now hold.

"No wonder Mom keeps all her memory cards so neatly labeled," Nolan says, his hands full of glossy prints. "This bin's a mess. Who even printed all of these?"

"I never knew we had them," Forrester admits. "Mom always said she wanted to scrapbook, though. She must have collected all our photos together, thinking she would do something with them."

We all crowd around the bin, pulling out snapshots and spreading them over the table.

"Wow, look at this!"

Hailey holds up a photo of Thomas and Nolan, when they were probably around six and three. Thomas has his arms thrown around his brother, and he's grinning at the camera while Nolan stares at the photographer in annoyance.

"Not much has changed." Allison smirks.

Nolan gives the photo a peevish glare, while Thomas laughs and takes the snapshot, pocketing it in his faded blue jeans.

"Here's one of you, Hailey," Forrester says, passing over a picture of Hailey sitting on a couch in a yellow sundress as she holds her baby sister.

"I've never seen so many actual pictures before," Hailey muses as she holds up the photo. "My mother always gets a few developed each year, but we're talking five or ten … there must be over a hundred here."

I paw through a series of photos full of people I don't know, before I glimpse one of Forrester and Eli building a sand castle on a beach. Allison is in the background, knee-deep in water, a lilac tutu around her waist and her head bent over the waves. I pass her the photo, and she snorts when she sees the image. I wonder what happened to the little princess I used to know.

"*These* are great photos," Eli remarks, sarcasm dripping from his tongue as he tosses one onto the middle of the table.

When I glance over, I see it's a shot from Uncle Joey's wedding. I study the photo of Joey and his new bride feeding each other wedding cake in outdated attire and then look up at Eli, confused by his nasty tone. Parents' wedding photos are supposed to be either sweet or embarrassing — either way, good for a chuckle. But Eli's not laughing at the pictures of his mom and dad. I catch the quick, solemn frown he exchanges with Allison before they both drop their heads and keep shuffling through pictures.

"Look at this one," Nolan says.

My attention is drawn away from the odd reaction of the twins as Nolan holds up a photo of my dad and his four brothers, all five standing around an old car. They're young, my dad in his early twenties, the youngest of the brothers — Hailey's father, Dean — in his early teens.

"Nolan, you look so much like your dad," Hailey says, sitting up on her knees and leaning over the table.

"Here's another one," Thomas adds.

He grabs a similar photo from the pile. Only this one includes an extra person, a teenage girl sitting in the middle of the boys. I figure it's a girlfriend, maybe one of my aunts at a young age. But then I notice something unusual about the girl. She has a small frame, and she sits in a wheelchair, gazing out at the camera with her body curled into itself.

She is not one of my aunts. She could have still been a girlfriend or a schoolmate, even a neighbor. But something about the girl makes my stomach tense.

I've seen her before.

No one speaks for several long seconds as we all stare at the image. Then Thomas lowers his head over the pile of photos scattered on the table.

"She's here, too," he says, holding up a picture of a young boy — one of my uncles, though I'm not sure which — next to a younger version of the girl.

"I've seen her," I say, the words slipping out before I can stop them.

I look at Thomas and then at Forrester and see recognition in their expressions as well.

"Who is she?" Eli asks, his chin resting against his fists and his elbows pressed into his knees. "I know I've seen her before, too, but I can't remember when."

"Christmas," Hailey says. She looks at Allison, and then back at the photo. "Not the one we spent here. But Christmas all the same. When we were, what, five or six?"

"I don't remember her," Nolan says, sounding bothered by his lack of recollection.

"Well, you wouldn't, would you?" Thomas replies. "Not if we were that young. You would have been two or three at the time."

Allison scratches her neck, her brows furrowed.

"I don't think I remember her, either," she says. She turns to her twin. "But you do?"

"Yeah, somehow I do." Eli nods.

I stare down at the photos on the table before grabbing another handful of images from the bin. Soon the others join me, our task now a purposeful one.

A familiar face in an old photograph is not problematic. But knowing the face without understanding *why* is. A name floats somewhere in the back of my brain, waiting to be drawn forward. I'm annoyed I can't latch onto it.

"Here's another one," Allison says after a moment.

Her fingers are pinched around the edge of a photo. She hands it to me, and I take hold of a faded picture of my parents with the girl. Mom's helping to wipe the girl's face, and even seated, it's easy to see she is pregnant — my older brother, Tate, squirming about under her rounded belly.

I drag my eyes back to the girl, her head tilted upwards while Mom cleans food from her mouth. A shudder runs down my spine, and I don't know why. I only suspect, with sad probability, there's something about the memory of this girl that frightens me.

I pass the picture to Hailey, and she studies it, her dark eyes narrowed.

"Christmas. Definitely Christmas. I remember a sweater, someone helping her open a sweater. And then, later, there was …"

"Screaming," Thomas mutters.

My head whips in his direction, my heart kicking against my ribs. Screaming. Yes. *Screaming.*

Hailey nods.

"Yeah. There was screaming, and I started to cry. And my mother picked me up and rushed me outside. I didn't even have a coat on, but she bundled me into her vest, and we waited until Dad came out with all our stuff. Then we went home."

"We went out for hot chocolate," Thomas says. "It wasn't Christmas Day, maybe Christmas Eve? Maybe even a few days beforehand. It was late, but the coffee shop was open. I remember I'd been scared by the screaming, but I felt a lot better once I got a drink and a cookie in me. Kayla, I think you and Tate came with us. I think maybe it had been at your house."

"And I didn't want to stay," I say, the memories forming like dense clouds behind my eyes. "I wanted my parents, but I didn't want to stay in the house, so I went with you. We spent a while away. And when we came back … she was gone." My brother lives in Ottawa now, but I wish he were here to tell us more. If I was five or six that night, Tate would have been eleven or twelve. He would remember better than any of us.

"I don't think I ever saw her again," Thomas says.

Hailey twists the wooden beads of her necklace as she shakes her head.

"I don't think I did, either." She glances at Allison and Eli. "You must have been there, too."

"I don't know. I'm not sure I remember the screaming," Eli says. "I just remember … her. Maybe we left early or something."

"Well, whatever happened, there had to be a reason for it," I say, sitting back against the couch. Looking at pictures was meant to be fun, but now I want nothing more than to stop. I cross my arms over my chest, cold despite the warmth of the room.

Hailey catches my eyes and sighs.

"I think we need a break," she says, pushing herself up and walking over to the kitchen. "What the hell do we have for food around here?"

We've been cleaning for an hour, maybe an hour and a half. Eli and I have sorted through three-quarters of the office's clutter, but there's still a closet packed full of stuff to go through. I don't mention this, though. A break sounds like too good of an option to pass up right now.

"Whatever's in the fridge," Forrester replies, his eyes still scanning the pictures.

"That would be ..." Hailey leans into the fridge, pushing around random items. "Um, nothing? Fuck, Forrester, don't you like to eat every now and again? There's hardly any food here at all, and nothing to drink."

Forrester looks up, unsurprised by her declaration.

"Must be grocery time." He shrugs, and I smile at the painless way he says it.

"Grocery time it is," Hailey agrees.

She heads toward the pile of bags we've stacked by the back door so she can grab her purse and the keys to her car.

ELI

Hailey, Thomas, and Kayla have gone.
Gone to get food.
Gone to escape.
Leaving the rest of us stuck putting away these old photos of
non-existent memories, timelines we've never been a part of.

I wish everyone would get a move on.
The faster we clean, the sooner we can go
home.

I don't know why Ali made me come.
Forrester's got enough help without me
and I had other plans.

The others believe
they can rekindle the fires
of youth
by being here together. Idiots.
Forrester's dad is dead. Do they really think
he cares about reminiscing?

My fingers linger on the last two photos to be placed back.
The first is Mom and Dad's wedding. I'm tempted
to crush it in my fist, tear it to pieces.

I curl my toes in anger instead,
let the photo drop,
careless,
back into the bin.

I stare at the other one,
five Hacher boys and one
mysterious girl.
I don't have a clue who she is, but there's something,

something —

Dad yelling.
Mom crying, and Dad yelling.

I place the photo onto the pile,
my breakfast threatening
to reappear
on the living room floor.

Thinking about Dad has that effect these days.
Trying to remember this woman doesn't help.

Swallow. Breathe. Stand.
I let Nolan close the bin, let Ali
move it aside, let Forrester
suggest we get back to cleaning.

I let them talk, but I don't join in. Not until I can get myself
   under control.
Swallow. Breathe.

Turn away so the others can't see how much
I want this weekend
to be over.

HAILEY

THE DRIVE TO TOWN takes about fifteen minutes. I keep my foot light against the gas pedal, my rusted yellow Ford slow to make each turn. Kayla sits beside me, and Thomas lounges in the back. None of us speak. We're too preoccupied with our own half-formed memories.

Of course I want to know who the hell the woman in the photos was, and why the hell she screamed. But traveling that train of thought makes me queasy. If she was a part of our family's life, at least between the time my dad was a teen and the year of the Christmas fiasco, I can't understand why I don't still know her now.

Another thought niggles in my mind as well, a recollection more recent and somehow connected. But I'm unable to push past the edges of it, to make out anything more than fluorescent lighting and a high-pitched giggle. I strain my focus until some asshole in a blue pickup blares his horn as he passes us. I roll down my window long enough to give him the finger, and then I shut off my brain and turn the stereo's volume up.

Buffy Sainte-Marie distracts me until we hit weekend traffic, where I'm forced back from outer space to navigate the stop-and-go push through town. A long sigh whistles through my lips when we find a grocery store and turn into the packed parking lot, circling around twice before managing to nab a spot. No one talks as the engine dies down, the music is cut off, and the doors are thrown open. I climb out, the sun bright and warm against my skin. I tilt my face into it and listen to the obnoxiously normal sounds of the traffic on the street behind us.

"Come on, let's get some food," I say at last.

We make our way toward the store, me in front, Kayla in the middle, and Thomas bringing up the rear. Inside is cool and crowded. I hate crowds. But it's Thanksgiving, so I guess I can't be too surprised.

"Should we split up, or tackle this row by row?" Thomas asks, while Kayla grabs a cart.

"We might as well stick together," she says. She tosses her sparkling teal purse into the cart and walks over to the produce area. "We're only buying enough food for today and tomorrow. How much could we possibly get?"

"Uh, haven't you ever heard of the Hacher appetite?" Thomas says, his eyes wandering even as he makes the remark. He checks out two girls buying apples, not the least bit shy when they notice his stare.

I give him a shove.

"Here for food, not for a date, eh?"

"Not looking for a date." Thomas grins. "Just looking."

I steer him toward the stand of oranges and bananas instead, and we pick a selection of fruits and cold cuts before an idea hits me.

"We should make a turkey," I say, watching the mass of people milling around the meat counter.

"You're kidding, right?" Kayla balks. "We can't make a turkey."

"Why not? It's Thanksgiving, isn't it?"

Kayla looks panicked. She turns to Thomas for support, but he only shrugs.

"Mom's a vegetarian, so we never have turkey," he says. "Only time I get it is as leftovers at someone else's house. Might be nice to have it fresh for a change."

My heavy braid slips from my shoulder and falls to the small of my back as I tilt my head in Thomas's direction.

"Your mom's a vegetarian?" I ask, interrupting my own conversation.

Thomas shrugs again. "Yeah. Has been since she was a teen. We're not, Nolan and I. Drives her nuts, but she doesn't push too hard."

"Huh, I had no idea."

Of course I had no idea. It's so fucked up, reacquainting yourself with someone you ought to be familiar with.

"Okay, but … *who* is going to cook a turkey?" Kayla asks.

She reaches a finger up to her face as if she's going to rub her eye, but her halt is abrupt, like she doesn't want to risk smudging her liner.

"I'll do it." I smile, ignoring the urge to rub my own eyes as a taunt. I like Kayla. I don't need to torment her. "I love to cook."

"Have you ever cooked a turkey?" Thomas asks.

This time I shrug. "No, but that's never stopped me before."

I head into the chaos, while behind me Kayla slumps over the grocery cart with a groan.

"This is going to be a disaster," she says.

I laugh to myself as I dig into a pile of turkeys, looking for the best choice. I pick a cook-from-frozen kind since we don't have a ton of time for defrosting. Then we head through the rest of the store, collecting the remaining ingredients.

"We'll make it easy on ourselves," I promise Kayla, trying to appease her fears about setting the cottage on fire or sending us all to the hospital with food poisoning. "Boxed stuffing and instant gravy. Frozen veggies, too. Okay? Except potatoes. I make a mean mash, but it's gotta be done from scratch."

"Sounds aggressive," Thomas says.

"It's kick-your-ass good." I smirk.

"What about dessert?" Kayla asks as we add a selection of beverages and some breakfast things to the cart.

"We need pie," Thomas says immediately. "It's not Thanksgiving without pie."

"I can't bake a pie," I warn them. "I can cook, but I can't bake to save my life."

"We can buy one," Kayla suggests.

Thomas shakes his head. "No way. The pie has to be real. I'll bake it myself if I have to."

"Can you bake?" I ask.

"Not at all," he says with beaming pride.

I roll my eyes as we turn into the next aisle. "*Great.*"

Thomas picks up a can of pumpkin, the kind with the recipe right on the label. We find the needed ingredients, and then further our gluttony by heading into the candy aisle.

This is my paradise. Other girls can diet all they want — I say to hell with it. If these last couple of weeks have taught me anything, it's that life can be shitty, so there's no point wasting it starving. I don't gorge myself on food. Lately, I've become much more aware of what I eat, and I try to keep it wholesome. But I have the fabled Hacher appetite, and I'm not afraid to indulge.

Only one person has ever had the gall to call me fat. She was in my sixth-grade class, and I poured fruit punch over her white pants and told everyone she'd gotten her period. I am, without question, capable of being a real bitch.

But at least no one calls me a pig.

"We have to have s'mores," I say as we pass the cookies. I don't even bother to check with the others before I grab two boxes of graham crackers from the shelf and then find the marshmallow packs.

"S'mores in October?" Kayla asks, heading toward the chocolate even while she questions my suggestion.

"Last ones of the year," Thomas sighs. "Winter will be on us soon."

"October only started a week ago — don't get ahead of yourself," I say, elbowing him in the ribs. "And why the long face?"

"I hate winter," Thomas replies. He sounds like a petulant child.

"I love it." I grin, thinking of roaring fires and snowflakes and cuddling hot boys for warmth.

"Enough talk of the seasons," Kayla says. "We have an important chocolate-related decision to make."

"Hmm, you're right," Thomas says, a serious look of consideration on his face as he approaches the shelf of chocolate bars. "What do we get: Hershey's, Jersey Milk, or Cadbury?"

"What decision? Jersey Milk is the obvious choice," I reply.

I reach for the chocolate, but Kayla stops my hand before I manage to put it in the cart.

"Um, no. Cadbury is way better," she says.

I gasp like she's just offended every one of my deepest morals. "You've got to be kidding me."

She shakes her head, reaching for the Cadbury chocolate.

"I kid you not. Nothing beats Cadbury. *Nothing*," she declares.

"I hate to mention it," Thomas adds, his voice meek, "but I like Hershey best."

"You traitor," I say at once, giving him a look of great disappointment.

"I honor my free will," Thomas replies in a dignified fashion.

I study the three choices and hold a hand up to silence the others.

"Guys, I have a solution," I say, waiting for their attention to shift back to me. "We can buy all three kinds of chocolate."

Kayla's nod is slow as she mulls over my proposal. "*All three kinds.* You know, I think you're on to something!"

"You beautiful genius, you," Thomas agrees, rubbing my head like I'm an obedient dog.

"Okay, let's grab all three, and we'll get some gummy worms while we're here," Kayla says while I fix my now-tousled hair.

She heads further down the snack aisle, tossing the chocolate into the cart. Thomas grabs a pack of Caramilk bars, throwing them over Kayla's head when she stops to pick out the next bag of treats.

"Three kinds of chocolate aren't enough?" I ask, grabbing a package of Starburst candies to accompany Kayla's gummy worms.

"For Nolan," Thomas explains.

"The perfect big brother." I smirk.

With the cart full of food, we line up for the register. We split the bill between us, Kayla paying cash, Thomas using his debit card, me loading up the Visa my mother doesn't know I borrowed from her wallet to hold me over until my next paycheck comes in. The cashier looks like she wants to hit us. I flash her my snarkiest grin as we collect our bags and leave.

Thomas takes over driving on the way back to the cottage. He turns the stereo off and rolls down all of the windows. I sit beside him up front, watching the town slip away as we head back out toward the bay.

"Do you think we'll get everything finished by tomorrow?" Kayla asks after we're out of town.

"We have to," Thomas says, but the edge in his voice betrays his worry.

"I had no idea there would be so much to do," I admit.

I think back to the bedroom with the stacks of receipts and cringe, imagining what the other rooms contain. No one managed to finish up an entire space before we took a break to look at the pictures. It doesn't bode well for the state of the rest of the cottage.

"Me neither," Kayla sighs from the back seat. "Can you imagine if Forrester had come up here all on his own? I can't believe his mom wouldn't make the trip, even if she does live in the States."

"No kidding," Thomas mumbles, flicking the car's signal to turn left. "I can't believe we didn't even know they were divorced. What a horrible situation for him. It's bad enough he had those two for parents in the first place. Then to be abandoned by one and have the other one die."

"What do you mean, it's bad enough to have had them as parents?" I ask.

"Don't you remember what they were like?" Thomas asks, glancing at Kayla in the rear-view mirror before giving me a sideways stare.

I shake my head and look back to see Kayla making the same motion. Thomas shrugs one shoulder as he faces forward again.

"I was only about nine the last time I saw them, so maybe I'm not the best judge. But it seemed to me Simon and Shirley were always … I don't know, selfish? I overheard my parents talking after the funeral. They were stewing about her absence, and my dad said that was what happened when marriage came from an unwanted accident."

"You mean they never wanted Forrester?" I shift in my seat so I can look at both Thomas and Kayla.

"Not at first, at any rate. Don't get me wrong, I think they loved him and all. I don't think they blamed him or anything. Or maybe they did, who knows? But I don't think they were fond of each other. Forrester was unexpected, and if he hadn't arrived, they never would have stuck together as long as they did. They weren't a family, at least it seemed that way to me. They were a mother and a father and a son, but not a family. And now Forrester doesn't even have the mother and the father anymore."

So I guess my memories are warped, at least a bit. The thought is fucking terrifying. I thought Forrester's parents were happy together, but Thomas's explanation makes sense. I think back to the same visions of the past I had last week when we sat around the picnic table outside the funeral home. Shirley was never outdoors with us. She didn't like the same things my uncle did.

Shit. My whole perspective's shifted in a matter of seconds. Makes me curious to know what other things I've gotten wrong.

The photo of the girl in the wheelchair burns like starlight behind my eyes, and as I hear the faded remnants of her screaming, I realize it's not just what I've gotten wrong, but what I've altogether forgotten, too.

"What will he do now?" I ask.

No one answers me. No point in mustering up a half-baked solution for a problem we're not equipped to solve. Forrester doesn't have much choice. He can keep living somehow. Or he can give up. I don't think he'll give up. But I have no idea how he'll handle the living part.

"We have to help him with this, even if we can't help him with anything else," Kayla mumbles after a moment. I nod, twisting one of the wooden beads on my necklace as I think of the cottage and the mess within it. "We'll have to work hard, is all," she continues. "And if we can't get it done by tomorrow, well … we'll have to come back. I can find the time, I'm sure. I can make the time, if I can't find it."

When we pull up to the cottage again, the sun is bright and the glistening water is tempting, even if it is too late in the season for swimming — even if I don't like swimming, anyway. I can still picture myself lounging around, reading a magazine and laughing at my cousins as they splash like frozen idiots in the water.

I want this to be a regular holiday break, a nice retreat with kids my age who are my friends, not just my relatives. I don't want death or screaming. I don't want confusion or fear. They don't belong here, not at this cottage.

They don't belong so close.

I help the others get the grocery bags, and we bring them inside.

NOLAN

Me: Okay, I've got about a
minute before I have to be
back upstairs.

B: You seriously have to be silent all
weekend?

Me: Yeah. They're into this
whole family bonding
thing.

B: Damn.

Me: I'll check in. I've got my
phone out of my cousin's
bag. She won't notice it's
gone.

B: Good. I need you for this.

Me: I'm here. Just might take
a while to respond. Are
you going to get the test?

B: Yes, leaving now.

Me: Good luck. Let me know
how it goes.

I'd better go back upstairs, I
only ran down to get a
garbage bag (you should
see the amount of trash
here).

Talk soon.

I don't hear the others return. After putting away the photographs, the four of us still at the cottage returned to the dizzying task of trying to get this damned place clean. I keep my phone away, only giving it the occasional glance as a reward for making headway in clearing the heaps of junkyard scrap and garage sale fodder my uncle could only have been keeping in preparation for building a demented funhouse.

Which is why Thomas catches me mid-text, my back to the door so I don't see him approach.

"I thought we took that away from you?"

I jump, startled by his voice and annoyed he's chosen this moment to slither in like a snake hiding in the trash.

"Shit, Thomas. You scared me." I give the phone a final glance before stuffing it in my pocket. "I was just checking for new messages, I swear. I've been working … see?"

I wave an arm around the room, prepared — if necessary — to show Thomas the honest-to-goodness box of chipped and tarnished porcelain-faced and floppy-bodied clown dolls I shoved into a garbage bag ten minutes ago. But Thomas isn't impressed by my efforts. He holds out his hand like I'm just going to hand over my most treasured possession.

"We agreed, no phones," he says. "How did you get it back, anyway?"

He steps toward me, and I step back.

"I retrieved it when I went down for a garbage bag earlier." I clutch a hand over my pocket in case he decides to lunge at me, a tactic not without precedent. "Let me keep it, okay? I promise I won't look at it in front of the others."

"*Nolan.*"

"It's important!" I meet my brother's gaze and glower with impatience. I don't want to tell him anything right now, but he's not leaving me much choice in the matter. "There's something going on, and I have to stay in touch."

Thomas leans back into a considering stance. "What is it?"

I press my lips together, not sure how to respond. I'm tempted to let him in, but there's nothing to actually let him in on. *Yet.* So, after a lengthy pause I shake my head, offering him an imploring stare.

"I can't say," I mumble. "But I promise it's important. Okay?"

Thomas's face clouds, and I know he's wondering since when do I keep secrets from him. Thomas thinks he knows everything about me, and for the most part, he does. I'm not one for secrets — at least, not for keeping secrets from him. But even I have a few hidden truths. And, it so happens, Brandon's latest messages make it necessary for this to be one of them.

"Fine," he says after an indecisive moment. His tone is resigned, and I do my best to ignore the whisper of disappointment within it. "But keep your phone hidden."

"I will, I will," I assure him. Then I push beyond our awkwardness by turning from his questioning gaze and reaching for a pile of old clothes lying on the bed. "These must be Shirley's," I say, picking up a glimmering dress.

"Either that or Forrester's got an interesting hobby he hasn't told us about." Thomas smiles.

I let out a snort of laughter, relieved he's making jokes.

"Good for him if he has," I say, holding the dress up against my gangly body. "But I'm not sure this would fit." The dress is tiny, a pink and slinky slip I'd expect to see on one of Thomas's girlfriends. Something I can only vaguely — uncomfortably — envision my aunt wearing.

Former aunt? Ex-aunt? What do you call the woman you were born knowing as your aunt, when she now lives in another country with another family and probably never thinks of you at all?

"Should we even bother going through these?" I ask, dropping the dress in favor of a semi-transparent blouse.

Thomas shakes his head. "Throw it all in a trash bag, and we'll take it home. We can drop it in a donation bin somewhere."

The plan works for me, although some of the outfits — like the black and white evening gown I can't understand having out here in the woods — would be better suited as costume pieces for a drama club or a film studio. When we sort the clothes at home, perhaps I'll pack some away for future video projects. For now, Thomas and I stuff around twenty outfits into a garbage bag, until at last the tropical print of the bedspread is uncovered.

"Eureka!" Thomas declares, making quick work of the last small objects scattered over the comforter. "We have a bed!"

I stand beside him, another full garbage bag in my hands and a small, stinging cut on my arm from — I'm sure — the edge of one of those damned, probably cursed porcelain clown faces.

"Well, look at that," I say, admiring the view. "Maybe this won't be impossible after all."

We clear out the room, tossing bags of junk over the balcony railing onto the first floor and pushing the remaining boxes out into the hallway so we can take them downstairs later. We're both sweating by the time we stop for lunch, and scarfing down a couple of sandwiches doesn't help us cool off.

"It's too hot in here," Thomas says, downing a bottle of lukewarm water and cursing the fact even his drink fails to be refreshing. "I think I'm going for a swim."

"Are you forgetting what month it is?" Hailey asks, gesturing to the fall leaves hanging from the branches beyond the windows. "I'm about to start the turkey. You don't cook Thanksgiving turkey and go swimming on the same damn afternoon."

"Sure you do." Thomas grins. He peels off his sweat-soaked shirt and heads for his bag. I'm astonished — and jealous — when he pulls out his swimming trunks. "Anyway, it's not cold. The bay will be fine."

"The bay will be freezing," Hailey retorts.

"The bay is always freezing," Forrester adds. He eyes my brother's bathing suit and lets out a soft breath of something close to laughter. "I'll join you. Last chance I'll have to swim here."

Thomas doesn't let the words sink us. He keeps his expression perky, digging through his bag again and pulling out another pair of shorts.

"Good. Nolan, you coming?"

He throws my bathing suit at me, and I stare at him in awe.

"Did you sneak into my room and steal my bathing suit?" I ask.

Thomas smiles in a way that suggests he may have invaded my privacy or he may have snatched the suit from the laundry room after the last time I soaked in the hot tub in our backyard. I wish I knew which it was. Thomas likes to tread a fine line between angelic and annoying. I try to stay a step ahead of his motives, so I know when to call him out on his bullshit and when to give him a silent moment of thanks for his well-intentioned interference.

We change and head down to the docks. I expect it to be just the three of us, but the others come outside, too. Well, some of the others. Hailey stays indoors, doing the prep work for the turkey, and Eli slumps away to keep cleaning. But Kayla sits cross-legged on the docks, and Allison surprises me by revealing her own black bathing suit underneath the baggy sweater she wore outside.

The bay is calm but not empty when I walk to the dock's edge. In the distance a canoe glides past us, two people-shaped specks soaking up the day.

I peer into the dark abyss of water, tempted to dip my toes in one by one. But all of us know the only true way to conquer the bay is to dive in headfirst. So I ward off my sensibilities and spring forward, reveling in the brief feat of flight until the frigid water crashes into me.

With the comfortable numb of initial contact keeping me subdued, I open my eyes to see nothing more than murk. Then the numbness wears away, and the cold pricks me all over as I glide up toward the promise of air. My head breaks through the water, the sun sizzling against my eyes.

"How is it?" Kayla asks.

My hair's flattened down over my face, and I push it back, working to keep my teeth from chattering.

"Freezing," I groan.

The dogs bark in unison as Forrester approaches the water.

"The way it's supposed to be," he says, nodding.

He gives me a small smile before jumping in himself, Allison a few paces behind him and Thomas joining us last as he cannonballs into the deep.

"Come on, Runner!" Forrester calls.

The huge dog races forward, his legs reaching a full gallop before he catapults off the dock. Runner slaps into the water and then paddles toward Forrester, at ease and evidently an expert at navigating the bay.

Star, meanwhile, takes a more reserved approach. Her tail wags like crazy, the force of it shaking her entire back half. But she doesn't venture into the water. Kayla gives her a pat, and the collie barks, circling twice before lying down to watch the rest of us swim and splash.

The bay is too cold to remain still, so I sink beneath the surface and stroke my way out past the shoreline. The muted rush of water in my ears is like the sound of tires rolling beneath a speeding car, the noise so constant it's almost silent.

When I pause for air, I'm not surprised to see that Thomas has passed me, while Forrester has left us both behind. His strong strokes make quick work of pulling his body out to the far reaches of the bay. I envy his ease in the water, the years of practice he's had in his own personal swimming hole.

Well, I almost envy it.

The reason we're here sloshes in my brain like water from the bay trapped between my ears. But even with the spike of guilt, the serenity doesn't fade. Before Uncle Simon died, this year was a good one with a decent winter and spring followed by the greatest summer of my life. If only the change of the seasons hadn't brought the bad news with it.

I watch Forrester swimming in the bay, and I recognize the languid way his body twists as he turns to the right. His father's dead, and there's a lot of pain and anger and desperation we don't see, a lot of shit we'll never understand if our lives are luckier than his. But in the water, he's let it go. He's not swimming with madness, not holding his breath in the hope he'll rise out of the water to see his dad waving from the shore. He's grieving, sure, but he's still living, too. He smiles at his dog, he almost laughs at our jokes. Little things I've so far failed to give any notice to. Moments I'll pay more attention to now.

This weekend is not about cleaning the cottage — it's about saying goodbye far too long before Forrester could possibly be ready. But he's trying. He's making his best effort at keeping himself afloat, and he's doing a damn good job of it.

I don't envy the life he's being forced to live. But I do envy my cousin's determination not to sink. Drowning would be easy. But he's not letting *easy* take hold.

KAYLA

THE BAY MUST BE too cold to swim in for long. After ten minutes of lazy paddling back and forth across the width of the cottage, Allison grabs hold of the underwater ladder and climbs out to join me on the dock. Runner scrabbles at the wooden planks, and Nolan pushes him up as best he can until the dog catches his footing and trots back toward the house. Star joins him, barking when he shakes his coat. I watch her bounce backwards to evade the spray, laughing at her agile avoidance.

"I can't believe we're a month into school when summer is still outside our door," I sigh as Allison sits next to me.

I wonder what Hudson's doing right now. The question is a torment, but I don't try to tamp it down. I can picture him back in Aurora, playing video games with his sisters or perhaps running a last-minute errand for whatever crucial item is missing for tomorrow's family dinner. My thoughts turn to Hailey in the kitchen, working to prepare our own feast. While I'm more than a little convinced our food will end up inedible, knowing we'll be having a family dinner of our own does — surprisingly — make the ache to be at home a little duller.

Allison pulls her towel tight around her lithe frame and crosses her ankles as she stretches her legs.

"It won't last," she says, glancing up at the sky. The sun is bright, but there are clouds scattered throughout the blue. "A storm is coming tonight. It'll change the season for us."

"You think?" I ask, my doubt obvious.

Allison's expression is that of an expert trying to converse with a novice — or an idiot.

"I know," she assures me.

"Know what?"

We both look behind us as Hailey steps onto the docks. Star keeps to her side, sitting when her owner stops walking. "Turkey's in the oven. Dinner is underway."

I smile, pushing aside my fears of burned poultry and soggy stuffing.

"Allison says the weather's going to cool off soon," I tell her. "I was saying it's tragic we're in school when it still feels like summer out here."

"Last semester I would have agreed, but I like school these days," Hailey says, sitting between us. Her hand moves to stroke Star's fur.

"You're a senior now, too, right?" I ask, and Hailey nods. "What made you change your mind about school?"

"Altered focus." She shrugs. "I thought I had a plan, and then I thought that plan had gone to shit. But then a new plan emerged, and it's motivated me to kick ass this year so I can get into the program I want after I graduate in the spring."

"What do you plan on studying?" Allison asks, her serious tone lightened with curiosity.

"Indigenous Studies," Hailey says.

I couldn't have guessed what she'd be interested in majoring in, but my cousin's response still manages to surprise me. Out of all the subjects Hailey or anyone else could choose to take, Indigenous Studies carries as equal a weight as everything else. But it's at odds with the Hailey I used to know. Once, when we were little, Hailey came to my house and we played with a couple of kids on my street. One of them said she didn't look like my cousin because she wasn't even white. Hailey punched him in the stomach and said she was. I'd never even thought about it before, and after that incident, I didn't intend to think of it again.

But of course, she's grown up now. Her life is different. It's been a long time.

Still, I or Allison or both of us must look intrigued, because Hailey stops petting Star and begins stroking her own long braid instead.

"Back in January, I'd had it with school," she admits. "I used to want to be a nurse, but I lost steam. I didn't finish my assignments and failed most of my tests. Which sort of put a damper on the whole career choice. I decided I wouldn't apply for anything after graduation — if I even graduated — but my mother refused to accept that. We got into a massive fight over it. She wanted me to go to university so I could have a better life than she did. She — you guys know she was born on a reservation, right?"

Allison and I both nod. I'm not sure why I know the fact, but it's been tucked in my mind all these years.

"Yeah, well, things weren't easy for her," Hailey says, as Nolan pulls himself onto the docks and is brought into the conversation as well. "I don't know the details, but I can make a few guesses. She left when she was fourteen and lived on the streets for a while in Toronto."

"She what?"

I had no idea my aunt was ever homeless. The thought sends a taut shiver down my back.

Hailey nods like she understands my reaction. "She ran away, changed her name, and did what she could to get by until an opportunity arose for her to make something of herself. She hates her past. All of it. She won't talk about her life before getting her first job and meeting my dad. I don't even know what her real name is — how fucked up is that?"

"She must have good reason to keep it buried," Nolan says.

Hailey shrugs him off.

"Yeah, I guess," she mutters. "Anyway, she kept bugging me to do some extracurricular things to make up for my lousy grades. She gave me brochures and website printouts for a whole host of weekly classes and summer camps. I was pissed off at her, so when I saw a summer camp that ran in conjunction with an Indigenous Studies program, I applied out of pure spite. She was livid. I only did it to annoy her, at first. But then I started reading about the camp, and, well, I kind of started reading about my heritage. The Cree part of my heritage, anyway. I never realized how fantastic and how awful it all is.

"I attended the camp this summer and loved it. I mean, it's overwhelming, and my mother still turns to ice whenever I mention it. But I know I want to enroll in Indigenous Studies, and I plan to be a sure candidate when I submit my application."

So that explains Hailey's changed appearance. I wasn't wrong to think it was unusual for her. Or, maybe unusual isn't the right word. Different? New?

I love the idea of Hailey claiming her heritage. But I hope it doesn't destroy her relationship with her mother.

Also, I can't believe I don't even know my aunt's real name. I wonder what kind of person she used to be — what her own family was like.

"Are you thinking about school, Kayla?" Allison asks, directing the subject to me. I blink out of my thoughts and stare at my cousin. "After high school, that is," she continues. "Do you know what you want to do once you've graduated?"

"Oh, um." I fumble with my words, feeling inadequate to discuss my studies after hearing Hailey's story. "I want to study history," I reply at last, flipping through a mental catalogue of all the schools I'll apply to in the next few months, and the only one I'm interested in attending. "I want to get my education degree so I can teach. You?"

"I haven't decided yet." Allison shrugs. She scratches at one of the swollen blemishes on her chin. "I'll go to school, but I don't know where yet. Maybe somewhere abroad."

"Really? Which country would you want to study in?"

I'd like to travel sometime, but the thought of going to school outside of Canada — outside of *Ontario* — has never occurred to me. Even if it weren't for Hudson, my heart would still belong closer to home.

"No idea." Allison's smile is dreamy as she closes her eyes and tilts her face into the sun. "I'm going to South America in March, if I can save up the money. I suppose I'll see if I like it. I'll apply to a few places in Europe. Australia, too, and who knows where else. I've been thinking I might explore Brazil."

"That's awesome. What about Eli, is he going to travel, too?"

Allison rolls her eyes at the question.

"He'll stay in Toronto," she answers in a clipped voice. "He plans to study engineering."

Hailey raises one eyebrow at her tone of disgust. "And that's bad because …"

"He's just doing it for the salary," Allison seethes. I get the impression this is an argument the twins have had before. "He has no actual interest in it."

I hadn't expected the question to cause such a heated reaction. I wouldn't have asked had I known.

"What would you rather he do?" Nolan questions.

"He's got a major talent for drawing, and a knack for design. He should be a designer or an architect or something. Not an engineer. He doesn't have a passion for engineering. He just thinks it will be an easy way to get a good career."

"Not everyone does what they love for a living," I say.

"Some people love stability and good pay," Nolan adds. "Not everyone wants to travel the world and live like a nomad."

Allison clenches her fists, her blue eyes dark. I wonder if Nolan meant to aggravate her. I can't quite tell if half of his utterances are said in earnest or if they are designed to annoy.

"I don't want to live like a nomad," Allison says, her words tight. "I want to study and make a career for myself. The difference is I want to do it studying what I love."

"School's overrated," Thomas says.

He bobs in the water, his arms folded on the dock. I don't know when he got back from his long swim out into the bay, but he's heard enough to understand the topic.

"You only think that because you barely finished," Nolan replies.

"Ouch, nice brother," Hailey says.

Nolan gives her an odd little smirk, somewhere between sardonic and proud.

"He's telling the truth," Thomas says with a laugh, as Forrester, back from his own swim, glides toward us and mimics Thomas's floating stance, "and I'm not ashamed of it."

With his arms exposed I can see his tattoos, two miniature landscapes of trees running the length of his inner wrists. They aren't identical, but they look like they're from the same original inspiration. They make me think of the painting in our kitchen at home, the one based on this very bay.

"I got through high school, which was torture enough," Thomas continues. "I couldn't pay someone for further misery on top of that."

"Yeah, but what are you going to do now?" Allison asks.

Thomas stares at the wooden planks in front of him, his black piercings and water-darkened hair a stark contrast to his light skin.

"I'm going to take a road trip," he says with a wistful smile. "I've gotten all I can out of this place, so I'm going to travel through Canada, the States — maybe even make it down to Mexico. See if I can discover something worthwhile."

"Dad and I were going to do that," Forrester says then, his voice quiet. Even in the sunshine, I can see what little color there is drain from his cheeks as he talks. "We were planning a trip for next year.

He said it was time to move on and let go. So, we were just going to pick up and leave. I think he needed to get away for a while. Things weren't going so well here."

"What do you mean?" Allison asks.

Forrester shrugs, pushing himself back from the docks amidst a rush of water.

"Business wasn't booming, no girl in his life ..." He pauses with a grimace. "His health hadn't been the best, either. He needed a break, is all. Guess he got one."

"Forrester," Hailey scolds.

He doesn't respond. Instead, he turns and swims away, leaving us to watch his retreat.

"What is he going to do?" I breathe.

Transfixed by the sight of his shrinking figure, I stare almost unblinking until Forrester's little more than a speck in the bay. Then I look around at the others. My cousins return my questioning gaze — all except for Thomas. He remains in the water, his body facing the distance, his eyes trained on Forrester.

"He'll be okay," he says after a moment, his voice firm. "Don't worry. He'll be fine."

I don't know what's going through Thomas's head, but his manner is so decided, all I can do is believe him.

THOMAS

FLOATING UNDER THE DOCK, whining boards and sloshing water add to the symphony of muted conversation.

"A trip."

"A trip? It's not possible."

"Of course it is. She'd like that, you know."

"Yes. She would. But I don't think it's possible, Simon."

Forrester calling to his dad, asking where the water toys ended up. Simon shouting a reply, believing me to be with him, stuck in the shed on the hunt for neon-colored plastic.

Me, below, wondering what trip and when, wishing I could go even if I didn't know where to or with whom. Wondering who she was and why a trip with her would be impossible.

Why any trip would be impossible. Why people couldn't always get up and leave whenever they felt it was time.

HAILEY

FORRESTER COMES BACK TO the cottage two hours after the rest of us have gone inside. I have no idea where he went. Swam to the other side of the bay, maybe. Or found a neighbor's canoe to take over to Huckleberry Island. Whatever the case, by the time he returns, we've packed up the boxes of stuff from upstairs to be driven back into town, and we've cleaned all of the upper rooms.

"Should we keep the boots or toss them?".

I lift an old pair of muddied boots, the black leather cracked and covered with a hard layer of brown muck. Kayla and I are now tackling the mudroom at the front of the cottage. I've already basted the turkey and prepped the side dishes for later. Thomas better come through with his promise of baking. I'm not going to have my dinner go unappreciated because everyone's too busy bemoaning the lack of dessert.

"Which ones are Forrester's?" Kayla asks, looking at the boots in my hand and the matching pair still on the floor. "We should get rid of Simon's. But Forrester might still want his."

I study the boots with a cringe.

"I can't even fucking tell," I say. Both pairs are old and disgusting. They look about the same shoe size, too. They must have been bought around the same time, probably after heavy tread wore holes in the bottoms of the previous pairs.

"Then again, he might not have much use for them if he doesn't have this place," Kayla muses.

She tilts her head to one side, the movement swirling imitation coconut and some kind of flowery perfume into the air. The scents are familiar. I used to buy the same sorts of products, before I decided spending money on manufactured smells wasn't the best use of my measly earnings.

My cousin and I used to wear similar perfume, and we used to be alike in other ways as well. Kayla's brown hair has been touched with highlights, and looking at it shine in the light through the mudroom windows makes me think of how I used to lighten my own hair — hating the thick black and wishing I could be a blond instead. She wears trendy jeans and a brand-name tank top, and I know how expensive the clothes are because I used to pine after the same labels. Makeup covers every pore of her face, and I remember the drawer of cosmetics I only convinced myself to throw away a couple of months ago.

Kayla hasn't changed. As a kid, she was never as girly as Allison. But as much as she liked digging for worms with the boys or walking through the woods with her parents and her brother, Kayla always had a soft spot for pretty dresses and bright shades of lipstick. For her seventh birthday, I bought her a beginner's makeup kit, and we painted and re-painted our faces for hours. I'm glad her personality has not flipped upside down, like Allison's. But although I love still being able to glimpse the girl Kayla used to be, it sort of makes me sick to see how readily she buys into the idea we need to spend money on false appearances to make us happy.

Of course, it's none of my damned business how Kayla lives her life — and who gives a fuck if she wants to wear three layers of makeup on a hot, sunny day. Kayla's not a bad person. She has a soft demeanor and a general complacency I envy. Wanting to look good doesn't mean she's selfish or cruel. Allison probably hasn't held a mascara wand her entire life, and her attitude is miserable.

Shit. I only gave up my nicest clothes a season ago, and already I'm so self-righteous I think horrid thoughts about someone else's appearance — while ignoring the fact I'm a total hypocrite, preaching simple living and then loading up a grocery cart with the kind of processed garbage I should be ashamed to eat.

Changing an entire outlook on life is hard. I didn't give up nice things for the sake of being an example of perfection. A purpose lies behind the uncluttered persona I still sometimes struggle to accept. Every time I think of buying new lipstick or an expensive bottle of lotion, I put the money I would have spent in a separate bank account. I'm not sure what I'll do once the funds add up to a worthwhile sum, but it will be something more important than splurging on a trip to the spa.

I study Kayla, both missing and hating the way I used to be. Both hating and admiring the way she is now.

"We could ask him, or we could get rid of the boots altogether," she says, oblivious to my silent judgments and internal accusations.

With a sigh, I grab a garbage bag and toss the boots inside before we spend any more time thinking about old footwear — and before I spend any more time thinking of how my cousin's lifestyle no longer aligns with my own. Forrester might be pissed if he ever notices the boots are gone. But they're gross, and he's not up to choosing the fate of every single item in the cottage, anyway.

Boots are boots. If he's upset, I'll buy him a new pair myself.

"I found Nolan trying to sneak a glance at his phone earlier." Kayla smiles as we dump the boots in the garbage. "He stole it back from my bag. He doesn't think anyone's noticed."

"He's pretty attached to that thing." I smirk.

She nods. "My dad would call it *smitten*."

My serious stare lasts for about half a second before I start to laugh. "Mine would say the exact same thing."

"They look alike, that's what's so weird about it," Kayla says, her face falling.

I glance at her, confused. "Who looks alike, Thomas and Nolan?"

"Well, yes, but no … I mean our fathers," she says. I drop the garbage bag and focus on Kayla's expression. Her brown eyes are sad, but the amber speck in her right iris still shines like a miniature star in the galaxy of her face. "They're all different, but they look so much the same," she explains. "At the funeral … at first I tried so hard not to look at Simon. But eventually I did. I saw him, and he looked ugly and dead. But he looked like my dad, too. He could have been my dad. He could have been yours. It's not like Simon was the oldest, after all. It's not like any of them are old."

"Grandma and Grandpa died young, too." The thought comes from nowhere, but I can't stop it getting loose from my tongue. "Young enough, anyway. We didn't even get to meet them."

"I know, it's so terrible," Kayla sighs.

"It's bullshit," I spit, my lips drawn tight. "It's bullshit for kids to not even meet their grandparents. And it's bullshit for a teenager to lose his dad." I pause, surveying the mudroom. "And it's bullshit that brothers have to get so worked up over some stupid piece of history they can't even be bothered to help clean up after one of them is gone!"

I kick the garbage bag at my feet.

"Your parents didn't offer to come and help, either?" Kayla asks.

"No, they didn't," I say. I expected they would, but I was wrong. "My dad barely made it through the stupid day, seeing his brother like that. But he's been so busy trying to decide what it all means to *him*, he hasn't given a single damn thought as to what it means for everyone else. My mother's shut herself off, focusing on Marissa and Liam and pretending nothing's happened. When I told them where I was going this weekend, they got mad at me for ditching work. Can you believe it? Because serving people burgers is more important than helping family."

"That's horrible," Kayla says, shaking her head. "But then again, mine weren't much better. They didn't get *mad*, but …"

She sighs, the tired gesture explanation enough. I offer a single nod of agreement before turning to leave the mudroom. My parents are messed up, but so are hers. It's not exactly a comfort, but there is some relief in not being the only one crushed with disappointment over the inaction of her creators.

I storm down the hall, but my temper cools as I pull open the door to the first-floor powder room and am confronted with the next task to accomplish. I'm grateful to see this room only needs a quick tidy. I'll deal with grease burns and pissy customers for hours without complaint, but cleaning bathrooms is not my idea of time well spent.

I wipe down the mirror, and Kayla volunteers to clean the toilet. Cleaning supplies are stashed under the sink, so once I've finished the mirror, I turn on the tap and swirl the water with foaming solution.

"Hailey, do you know anything about what tore them all apart?" Kayla asks as I stare at the porcelain before me. Her words are a continuation of the conversation I tried to abandon in the mudroom, and the question is equal parts unexpected and anticipated. After all, I asked Allison the same thing only a couple of hours ago.

"My dad said something about family, once," I mumble. I didn't tell Allison this. I didn't think of it until now. Maybe Kayla's drawn it out of me because she feels less like a stranger. "I know that sounds pointless … a family fight being about family, big fucking surprise! But he wasn't talking about his brothers. He said something about someone *not* being family. I can't remember much about it. It was years ago, I guess right about the time the fight happened. My parents thought I was asleep, and they were arguing. My mother said something about having sympathy, and my dad said he did, but that it wasn't his fault, and it didn't change anything."

"Did they say anything else?"

Kayla finishes scrubbing the toilet. I turn off the tap and eye her in the mirror.

"No." I shake my head and bend forward to wipe down the sink.

"Liam started crying, and my mother left, and my dad turned on the TV. And then I guess I probably did fall asleep. It doesn't help much, but I used to be curious who he was talking about."

I'm curious about it now, the old scene playing through my head as I clean the sink and dry it off with paper towel. Shit, I hate the heaviness of this whole weekend. I didn't expect two days of sun, sand, and fun, but I didn't plan on feeling so many ups and downs all weekend, either. I want to call one of my hookups. Damien, maybe. He's so self-centered he wouldn't ask how I was feeling or whether I wanted to talk about it. I'd like the distraction of his pushy hands and skilled tongue.

But he's at home, as likely as not hungover and maybe using his skills on one of the other girls he thinks I know nothing about. So, I stuff the remaining paper towel back under the sink and follow Kayla out into the hall.

If my dad and his brothers hadn't fought — if they'd stayed a happy family — things would be so much different now. Shirley might still have left, but at least Simon wouldn't have let his health suffer if he'd had the support of his brothers and the company of everyone around him. Or, maybe I know fuck all, and he really was supposed to go when he was supposed to go. But even if he was destined to die, the aftermath would make more sense if my eighteen-year-old cousin didn't have to be so damn alone.

Mental powers tingling, I walk into the living room and see Forrester standing in the back doorway, a towel around his waist, his hair wet and clinging to his face. His eyes are obscured by the fringes of his bangs, and I can't tell what he's looking at. I hope it's not at me. In this moment, I can't fake a smile or attempt a lighthearted remark about his dripping a puddle of water on the wooden floor. If I try to open my mouth now, I'll say something stupid. Or worse, I'll start crying for no fucking reason at all.

My problems mean jack. He's the one with something real to

cry about, and he's standing across from me, trying to keep himself together. I refuse to be the cause of him losing the few stitches he's managed to sew.

"Dude, I just scrubbed that floor so hard I could see my reflection in it," Thomas says, his voice deadpan.

He stands in the kitchen, and his words surround me like a comforting blanket. No more thanking the stars for Thomas. I'm going to have to give my thanks to *Keesik Aski* — the entire sky world.

"Sorry." Forrester shrugs.

He offers Thomas a wry smile before dashing across the living room and taking the stairs up two at a time. I swallow down breath after breath, staring at the water on the floor as I wait for my nerves to settle. I stand like that until Forrester reappears on the upper balcony, his hair still wet but his bathing suit exchanged for dry clothes.

"Better?" he asks.

Thomas offers an approving nod.

"Okay," I say, dropping our mudroom garbage bag by the back door as I force myself to get a grip on my sappy sentimentality. I cross the room and step down into the sunken square of the living area. "I think we've covered this storey." Flopping onto the couch, I peel a couple of hair ties off my wrist before pulling free my braid and looping the hair into two quick pigtails hung low against my shoulders. "What should we tackle next?"

"Well, it might be best to get the shed out of the way," Forrester suggests as he bounds down the stairs. "Before it gets dark."

I slump into the cushions, my nose wrinkled. "I was hoping you'd have forgotten about the shed."

"You've always hated it out there." Kayla smiles. "When we used to play hide-and-seek, the shed was the safest place to hide when you were the one in charge of seeking."

"It's full of bats," I grumble.

"And bugs," Allison adds, her voice tinged with excitement.

I quirk a brow at her interested expression.

"You hated the bugs," I remind her.

Allison blushes. "I thought I was supposed to," she mumbles, her tone almost apologetic. "I thought girls had to be afraid of bugs."

"I take it you're not afraid of them now?" Thomas asks.

Eli scoffs. "Ali's not afraid of anything. You should see her collection of snail shells."

"Ew, snails?"

I give her a disgruntled look, and Allison smirks.

"They're gorgeous creatures," she says.

"They're *gross*," I argue.

"They're *beautiful*," she says with a serious edge.

"They're delicious," Thomas pipes in.

"You've never had snails in your life," Nolan says.

"Fine. But I'm sure they'd be delicious," he amends.

Allison scowls at him. Sweeps of blond hair have escaped from her ponytail, and she brushes the strands back behind her ear.

"You're as bad as Nathan," she mutters, tugging at the bottom of her sweater before she heads for the back door.

"Who's Nathan?" I ask, my smile mischievous.

"A friend," Allison says.

Eli snorts, and Allison turns her glare on him.

"What, have you broken up again?" he asks.

Her cheeks flush an angry pink.

"Maybe we have," she snaps. "So what?"

"For fuck's sake, Ali." Eli looks pissed at his sister, and Allison's boyish body tenses under his remonstrance. "Let the guy go, will you? You break up with him every other month, and then give into him and start dating again."

"It's none of your business," Allison seethes.

"You don't care about him, and he's mad about you. Give him a break!"

I'm torn between regretting my question and loving the sibling drama now unfolding before us.

"I care about him plenty," Allison replies. She sounds almost hurt by her brother's comment, which is surprising after all of the furious back and forth between them. "But I don't love him, and he knows it. When he gets too close, I break it off. He understands the drill, and if he wants to go through it all again, why should I care? It's not like I'm —"

She trails off as Eli's stare flashes in warning.

"It's pretty much the same damn thing, Ali," he growls.

Allison blinks, her eyes glossed over with unshed tears.

"I can't believe you'd say that," she mumbles, her voice tight.

Eli shrugs, turning his back on her. His shoulders are tense as he leaves the house, and I watch him through the windows until he curves out of sight, headed in the direction of the shed. Allison stands in the living room for a moment, wiping her eyes with the backs of her hands. She doesn't look at any of us. She stares after her brother too, and then follows him outside, the back door slamming shut behind her.

"What the hell was that all about?" Thomas asks.

I glance around at the others, unable to hide my amusement. I'm used to temper tantrums. I've thrown enough of them myself, and I've got two younger siblings to boot.

"Should we join them?" Kayla asks, uncertain.

She's not sure if it's acceptable for us to interfere with their fight, and she doesn't want to be rude. But I'm not about to let two bickering siblings delay the work we have to finish on a tight deadline. I'm kind of interested to find out more, anyway. I want to know what secret these two have been keeping.

"Yeah, let's go," I say, my voice dripping with disdain only partially forced. "Let's tackle the stupid shed."

ELI

Great. Now we look like stars of our own daytime soap.
Me and my
stupid temper.

I can't help myself.
Ali's one step away from ruining that boy's life
with her careless
attitude, her lack of regard for the
fragility
of his heart.
She's one step away from being like Dad, and I can't deal
with two of them
in one family.

I don't think she gets it.
If she ends up like him, I'm cutting her out.
I don't want to lose my sister, but I've got enough shit to
stress about
without the chaos
of her mistakes.

I wish she'd stop dragging Nathan around
like some kind of sad teddy bear.
Maybe it'll happen soon. One more year

and they'll be forced to separate.
Ali wants to travel. He won't follow her from country to
  country,
hanging around while she studies insects
and chases after storms.

At least,
I fucking hope
he won't.

It's still only the afternoon.
Time is creeping

like one of the bugs in the shed.
I'm so sick of being here,
being stuck
somewhere me and my sister
can't even
properly
fight.

I'm sick of these people I don't care about
being so near
the embarrassing drama
of my life.

One more day.
By this time tomorrow, Dad will have picked Ali up.
I'm not happy with the arrangement. It's a waste
of time and gas money for us to leave separately.

But at least it means I'll be free
to go home alone.

Twenty-four hours,
and I can leave this place
for good.

KAYLA

THE MID-AFTERNOON SUN SHINES bright and warm as we join the twins by the shed. Allison leans against the wooden boards painted in peeling white, while Eli is slumped to the ground, his finger tracing absent shapes in the dirt by his feet. They're both silent, their lips drawn in identical tight lines. As I approach, I stare away from them, studying the shed to avoid making any awkward eye contact.

Luckily, the shed, like everything else here, offers enough in the way of memory to distract me. Even as I turn to study its worn exterior, an old thought flickers in my head, and despite the gravity this moment should be settled in, my cheeks flush with happy embarrassment as a muted giggle escapes my throat.

Forrester's glance is perplexed, but his confusion only makes me laugh harder.

"What's so funny?" Hailey asks.

I wave her question away, trying to straighten my lips into a serious line.

"Nothing. It's nothing." I look at Forrester and lose the battle against my grin. "The Shed People," I say.

It takes only a few seconds before he, too, breaks into a smile. A *real* smile, one reaching all the way to his eyes. For the look alone I want to hug the shed and its childish recollections.

"I still can't believe how much that freaked you out," he says, remembering the incident as quickly as I did when I took in the shed's old, familiar shape. "It was the dumbest lie I could have told you, and

I didn't even mean for it to be scary."

"Who are the Shed People?" Allison asks.

Her eyes are tired, and the coloring in her cheeks is off, but she and Eli are not, for the moment, yelling. Her twin doesn't look at us. He keeps his head down, his finger still trailing designs in the earth.

"I told Kayla that people lived in this shed," Forrester explains. This memory is one of the few I have of the cottage that the others are not a part of. We didn't always spend time here as a complete extended family. Sometimes Forrester would have been here with only his parents, and sometimes just one or two of his uncles would have made it up for a week or even a weekend. "I said they only came outside at night, so we never got to see them. And she got massively scared."

"Think about it. Creepy night dwellers stalking about in the dark. It's like vampires or something," I say, trying to defend my pathetic childhood delusions. I think about the nights I spent watching the stairs leading down to the basement, sure someone was sneaking around the cottage in the dark. Even now, I can't sleep without the curtains drawn over my window at night. I have a paranoid suspicion I'll look over to see someone standing outside, despite the fact my room at home is on the second floor.

"Speaking of vampires," Thomas says. He motions toward the shed, where Runner and Star are sniffing at the door. "Look, Hailey, there's probably something living in there now. Maybe Kayla's fears were well founded."

Thomas pokes Hailey in the back, and she shudders. She calls to Star, and the collie obeys, her tail wagging as she comes to rest by her owner's side.

"You've got your protection," Forrester assures her. "You'll be fine. If there is anything in there, Runner will chase it out."

"That's a great comfort," Hailey mutters.

Forrester approaches the door and reaches up to grab the key from the inner lip of the overhanging roofline. Not the safest hiding place for the shed's only key, but in one of the rare landscapes where people still leave their doors unlocked all summer, it seems more than adequate to place a padlock on the shed and hide the key out of sight.

Forrester twists the lock and pulls open one half of the shed's double doors. Runner bolts into the dark, and even Forrester disappears into the shadows for a moment before a shot of light from a lantern hung just inside the doorway brightens the shed's front end.

Star whines by Hailey's side, and with a resigned sigh Hailey gives her a pat on the head.

"Go on," she says.

The collie bounds into the shed to join Runner's explorations.

"Let's get started," Forrester suggests.

He waves us all inside. Allison follows first, while Eli remains seated on the ground until a few others have passed, forcing a distance between him and his sister.

I wonder what their fight was about. Obviously, the anger exchanged between them results from a matter of the heart, something deeper than Eli's annoyance of Allison's on-again, off-again boyfriend. Their harsh words did not spark the first tense moment since our arrival here, either. Something major is simmering, and I wish I were a little bolder so I could barge into their personal space and demand to know what it is.

Of course, I'm not the kind of person who could help them, anyway. I'm okay at observation, but problem solving is not a skill set I possess.

I wait until Eli's in the shed before I step in myself, Nolan trailing behind me. Inside is dark and dank, the air full of the musk of damp earth and the moist collection of old dust.

"Isn't there a window in here somewhere?" Hailey asks.

The flicker of a smile crosses Forrester's face as he walks past the light of the hanging lantern. The clattering roll of a shade being pulled up further disturbs the stale air, and soon streams of dusty light filter in across the middle of the large shed's interior.

"Better?" Forrester asks.

Hailey nods, casting a disgruntled look about her and making no effort to move from her spot near the doorway.

"Yeah, but let's get this over with quickly, okay?" she says.

"You don't have to join us," Nolan says with a sympathetic glance. "You can wait inside and do some more cleaning. I'm sure someone would go with you if you wanted. We don't all need to be in here."

"Yeah, but it's fun," Allison says, walking into the shed until she reaches a plastic bin with a warped cover. "This is where the good toys were always kept."

"True," Thomas says, approaching the tarp-covered canoe held off the ground by a couple of wooden sawhorses. He looks over his shoulder at Forrester. "Please tell me we can take this out tomorrow morning. A sunrise trip? That would be awesome."

"Sure," Forrester agrees. He lifts the tarp back, running his hand over part of the canoe's side. "I've got to take it out and strap it to the car, anyway. I'm bringing it with me. We only got it last year. Dad always wanted a proper cedar canoe, and we finally splurged on one."

Forrester doesn't sound sad when he says this, and his eyes gleam with fondness as he stares at the canoe. At least, even with the cottage sold, he'll be able to take some piece of this place with him. He could even drive up here, canoe the bay, paddle right past the docks and see the cottage again if he ever wanted to.

Okay, so maybe coming back here would be the worst thing he could do. But Ontario is home to many lakes and rivers begging to be explored in a crafted vessel like the one in this shed.

Thomas studies the canoe with as much awe as Forrester.

"Now this would be a great way to see the country," he says after a pause, his voice full of consideration. "Strap this onto the car and use it whenever possible."

"That would be perfect." Forrester nods.

He looks at Thomas, and the two share a glance that holds a meaning I do not understand. As far as outward appearances go, these two share little in common aside from their related facial features. Forrester is more athletic, raised lakeside in the summer and snowy hillside in the winter. I don't know how much time Thomas spends outdoors, but his personality is from the city, with his edgy attire, his loud attitude, his ability to jump into any situation whether he's invited or not.

But they're sharing something here. I glance over at Nolan, who's looking around the shed, unbothered by his brother's comments and unaffected by the conversation at hand. He doesn't possess the same spark of yearning as the other two. I turn my gaze to Allison, who's moved on to her own study of the shed. Thomas and Forrester's shared desire has nothing to do with a love of travel, either — it's something deeper, more fragile — and perhaps more painful, too.

"Hey, Kayla, remember this?"

I follow the sound of Eli's voice, breaking from my thoughts and making my way over to where he squats wiping grime off an old pile of wood lengths. It looks like nothing but trash, pieces well rotted and unfit even for burning. But the sight of them brings me right back to the day they were stored in the shed, tucked into a corner and covered with a promise of future uses to come.

They were put here the last time I visited this place.

"Our fort." I smile.

I remember the week when my dad and Uncle Joey occupied this place alone, while Forrester's family was on a vacation extending further than the cottage. A neighbor had been demolishing part of their own property, preparing to add an additional room. Our dads helped clear away the junk, and they rescued a few bits of wood for us to play with.

"That was the worst fort ever," Eli says with a rare grin. "But it was the best."

Eli designed the fort, and together with our dads and my brother we both helped to build it. Allison had been intrigued in the beginning, but soon her attention was drawn away by the chance to chase rabbits through the woods and go fishing with her mom. The construction of our fort was crude at best, nails hammered into wood and shaped into a simple box structure leaning against the base of a tree not far from the cottage's front door. But we loved it, and once it was complete, we played in it non-stop until the week ended, the fort was dismantled, and our fathers assured us of a future rebuild.

I wish we could rebuild it now. If we had fresh materials and some extra time, I'm certain this is one activity Eli would have no qualms about participating in. But we have neither of those things, so all we can do now is clear the wood out of the shed to make the space more presentable for sale.

The first storage bin Allison spotted has goggles, snorkeling gear, old foam pool noodles, and a variety of plastic balls used for throwing around in the bay. After we get the woodpile out, Thomas and Nolan pull out a second bin of swimming accessories, and Hailey takes great delight in staying out in the sun to sort both bins' contents into what can be kept and what unquestionably has to be tossed away.

We leave the life jackets strung up from the shed's rafters, and for the moment we leave the canoe on its base as well. A couple of ladders, old paint cans, and some tools line the back shelf, along with bundled camping gear, a rusted old patio set, and a few boxes of random household items stored away and forgotten over time.

We sort the remaining items, clearing out the garbage and leaving the tools likely to be useful to anyone purchasing the cottage. A small trailer is stored around the shed's side, and Thomas and Forrester attach it to the back of the old Jeep so we can load the junk up, ready to be hauled off to the dump.

When we're finished clearing the big items, we stand near the back of the shed, organizing the rear shelf and surveying the rest of the shady space.

"I think that's it," Thomas says at last.

I nod, glancing at Forrester for approval to move on. He nods as well, but then something catches his eye, and he grabs at a sign hanging on a nail in the back corner next to the ladders.

He brings it over, and in the light of the window we see it's a piece of wood with words painted in all capital letters.

SKIS IN ATTIC.

"I suppose we have our next task," Nolan says through a tired breath.

The sun is still shining, but it's almost five now, and the day's work has been more than enough for all of us.

"Let's get it done while there's still light," Allison says, sounding decisive. "Then we'll have dinner."

"Speaking of which," Hailey yells from outside, "Thomas still needs to bake us a pie!"

Nolan laughs — full-out laughs — his expression gorgeously bright with amusement.

"Thomas is going to bake?" he asks, turning to his brother. "You have to promise I can film the entire thing."

Thomas gives him a shove. "So you can capture my debut as a world-famous pie maker?"

"Something like that." Nolan smirks.

"Okay, well, let's do the attic quick, and then Thomas can delight us all in the kitchen," Allison repeats.

"We can do the basement tomorrow," Forrester agrees, looking at us with a sorry — but grateful — expression. "We can spend the rest of tonight relaxing."

"Sounds perfect," Hailey says from her post in the doorway.

Star and Runner sit on either side of her, their fur covered in dirt, their eyes shining with joy.

HAILEY

FIRST THE SHED, NOW the attic. Fuck. We can't even bring the dogs with us this time, so if a bat starts swooping around hell-bent on giving us rabies, we're screwed. No one else seems to care about our well-being, and I've already acted enough like a chicken. I won't complain again. But I'm not happy with the arrangement. Blood, guts, and all kinds of sick I can handle. Critters, on the other hand, need to stay well out of my way.

I've never been into the attic at the cottage. I didn't even realize there was an attic to enter. I guess if I had ever stopped to think about it, the existence of an attic would seem plausible. But until today, it never occurred to me a ladder was folded up atop a hatch in one of the spare bedroom's closets.

Stepping up the ladder rungs is a careful process, the wood rough and weak beneath my touch. Forrester, Thomas, and Eli have already gone up, each of us ascending one at a time in case the thin ladder can't hold the weight of two bodies. As my sights pull away from the bedroom and move up into the attic, I expect darkness. Instead, I'm relieved to find a bright, open room.

The attic covers only half the width of the entire cottage, and there are large windows on either side of the slanted ceiling to let in the full strength of the remaining daylight. While the space is not massive, it is cleaner than I imagined. The windows are nice, too. They make me think of the telescope my mother has in the study at home. I'm surprised she never brought the instrument here. We've spent many nights watching the stars together — one of the *very* few interests we share — and this would have been an excellent place for gazing.

"Why do you have skis up here, anyway?" Thomas is asking when I climb up onto the attic floor. "Wouldn't you keep those in town with you?"

"These ones are for cross-country skiing," Forrester says. "We didn't go all that often, but sometimes we'd spend an afternoon in the woods. Dad kept all the winter stuff up here."

The skis rest against the back wall, along with pairs of snowshoes and several winter jackets hung up on hooks. I spot fishing gear, too, and one of those classic wooden sleds for tobogganing.

"Did you come up here in the winter often?" Kayla asks, crawling up behind me. "I don't remember many winter visits."

"Sometimes. Depended on the year, on what conditions were like. Last winter we didn't come up here at all. Dad wasn't too well. My mom ... she liked this place in winter, actually. She thought it was romantic. After she left, we didn't come up as much."

"Have you talked to her in the last week?" I ask, my words measured. "Does she know what's been happening?"

"We talked a couple of nights ago." Forrester shrugs, turning away from us and heading over to the sporting equipment. "She offered for me to come down to Colorado, but I don't think she really meant it. Kept stressing how crowded the house would be."

"Have you even met the new guy? Your, well, I guess your stepdad? And you said he had kids, right?"

I'm too curious not to press. I want to know what's become so damn important in Shirley's life she can't even be here for her only child. Only biological child, at least.

Forrester takes down the winter coats, throwing them toward the ladder just as Allison ascends.

"I met him, once," he says while Allison ducks out of the way. "Three or four months after she moved out. She wanted me to drop off a few of her things. She was staying at his apartment, and when I got there, he was leaving for work. It was … awkward. He seemed about as interested in me as I was in him. I've never met the kids, though."

"I still can't believe it," I snarl. Everyone's up in the attic now, and the others all stare at Forrester's back, unsure how to react to his story. I seem to be the only one capable of making any comment. "I don't understand how she can be so horrible."

"It's not her fault," Forrester says, picking up the sled. "We were never close. Even as a kid, I always spent more time with my dad. When I got to be a bit older, I realized I didn't even like her much. She was so … fake. All she ever wanted was to look nice, to have nice things — to be important. She was the type of woman who woke up before my dad every morning just to do her hair and put on some makeup so he wouldn't see how she really looked. Dad never even noticed. I doubt he would have cared one way or the other."

I glance at Kayla. I don't mean to, but I can't help it. She loved Aunt Shirley when we were kids. Me, Kayla, Allison, and Shirley would play dress-up together, and our aunt would let us wear real makeup when the other mothers weren't around. Kayla looks stricken by what Forrester's said, and I'm curious if any boyfriends of hers have ever seen her without a perfect face and clean, sleek hair.

"Still," I say, forcing my eyes back to Forrester.

He glances over his shoulder, cutting me off with a fierce look.

"No, it's not her fault," he says again. His already dark eyes are further shadowed in the recesses of the attic. "She is who she is, and I can't blame her for that. It's not always like it's supposed to be. Happy family and all. We were used to each other, and I did believe we'd always be together — but that didn't mean we worked. Her leaving made sense. It was a shock, but even when it first happened, I knew it made sense."

"So, you won't go and stay with her," Kayla says, her voice heavy with emotion.

Forrester may have been unaffected by the life he experienced with his mother, but that doesn't mean we have to be. I can't stand my mother most of the time, but it'd be awful to live so far away from her, a country apart and totally detached. Of course, my mother *did* leave her home, so maybe she'd understand how Forrester feels. As far as I know, she's never spoken to anyone from her reservation since the day she fled. I wonder if she ever misses it, or if she's cold to the idea of sentimental feelings left over from a life abandoned.

"I won't," Forrester agrees.

The others have nothing else to say. I could still pick out a few unpleasant utterances, but I've annoyed him enough already, so I let the attic sink into silence. For a moment, I close my eyes against the sight of my cousins. When I open them again, it's to see Thomas crossing in front of me, heading over to help Forrester with his work.

"Doesn't look too bad in here!" He smiles, pretending the story hasn't been told, the sad facts not revealed. "Shouldn't take us long at all. Which is good. I'm getting hungry."

"Let's get to it, then," Eli says.

Soon, we're all moving again, the sounds of shuffling feet and shuffling objects bringing the attic to life.

The shed was far more crowded than the attic is, making this final task for tonight blissful in comparison. I'm hot and tired of cleaning. I know there's still more to be done, but we've been at it all fucking day, and I'm ready to mash potatoes in the kitchen.

We start with the equipment hung up against the wall.

"No need to keep this stuff here," Forrester says, looking more tired than the rest of us. "I'll pack it up and bring it home. I can figure out what to do with it all later."

Thomas descends to the cottage's second storey, and we lower the fishing poles, skis, and sled down through the attic floor. Once they've been taken care of, he comes back up so we can chuck everything else through the opening.

"We'll sort it after," Forrester says, and without hesitation we all agree.

A few minutes of active work and the attic's clear except for three boxes tucked into the far back corner that we almost miss. Nolan's the one to see them, catching the half-hidden containers on a final walkabout.

"There are some boxes here," he says, grabbing hold of a standard-variety brown cardboard box and dragging it out into the middle of the room. "They're not heavy," he adds, glancing back at us before fetching the next one.

"Must be some old clothes or something," Forrester says, his voice revealing a note of confusion.

Thomas joins his brother and pulls out the final box. I walk over to them, prepared to open the flaps and find bulky sweats and snow pants folded away for the cold temperatures of the coming months.

The boxes have no descriptions on them, save a name on the top of each written in a careful, though still messy, hand.

Julie.

"Who's Julie?" Kayla asks.

Forrester shrugs, looking more perplexed than before. "I have no idea."

He bends down next to one box, pulling at the edge of the tape sealing it shut while Thomas uses his keys to pry off the tape on the second one and Allison uses some kind of penknife to slice open the third. Inside of all three boxes are clothes — women's clothes, which makes sense, given the name written on the top.

"I don't know any Julie," Forrester says as he paws through the clothing.

Whoever packed these boxes didn't do so with order in mind. T-shirts, jeans, sweaters, shorts, an old nightshirt, a bathing suit, and a pair of running shoes are mixed together without rhyme or reason. In the third box, there is even a pink teddy bear and a small wooden jewelry chest that seems to have lost its key.

"Could she have been, well ..." Allison trails off and looks at her brother.

"A girlfriend of your dad's?" Eli finishes.

Forrester's quick to shake his head, his brows drawn low.

"No," he says. "Dad didn't see anyone after Mom left. Romance wasn't his area. And if he did have a girl up here, he would have told me. Wouldn't be any reason not to. We didn't keep secrets from each other."

"Unless he had a reason for keeping it to himself," Kayla says, her voice unsure.

I look at the clothing and shake my head as well.

"No," I say, bending down over one of the boxes. "Look at all this stuff. It's old." I pull out a large T-shirt with a cartoon moose on it. "These have been well worn — and look at the jeans." I grab a pair of faded jeans, the waist small, the hips wide, and the pant legs straight. "These look like something from the early nineties."

"So, what is it doing up here?" Kayla asks.

I take out a sweatshirt from Canada's Wonderland, a pair of jean shorts, and a shirt with a flowered design on it.

"Yeah, why keep a bunch of old clothing from someone we don't know?" Thomas murmurs.

"Could it be someone from your mom's side of the family?" Nolan asks.

"Mom's an only child," Forrester mutters. "And her mother's name is Vera."

"Well, maybe it was a friend," I offer. "Someone your parents knew, maybe someone with a cottage up here. They could have been storing the stuff, and then it could have just been forgotten ..."

My words taper off as my eyes take in the brown and green wool sweater Thomas has pulled from the second box. I drop the shirt I'm holding and sink to my knees, landing too hard. Pain throbs through my kneecaps. I'd let loose a few curses if I wasn't so stunned.

"What's the matter?" Allison asks, looking between us.

Thomas holds the sweater up, showing it first to me and then to Kayla. Once more the image we ignored for so many years reappears, and along with it comes the fuzzy static of my other memory, the fluorescent lights and giggles I still can't place.

"The woman," Kayla says, sucking in a breath.

"What woman?" Forrester asks, his words sharp with impatience.

"The screamer," I mutter, and then the others understand, at least as much as they can without the memory to aid them.

The woman from that Christmas, the one in the photos we found earlier, was Julie. And for some unknown reason, Julie's clothes have been stuffed into boxes and crammed into the corner of a cottage attic. A cottage owned by a man now dead. The clothes aren't modern, and the boxes they are packed in are coated with a thick layer of dust. They've been up here a long time.

But these newest pieces of information explain nothing — only make everything about as clear as the mud we used to track in from outside. I hate mud, and I hate knowing fuck all about what's going on.

"It still doesn't explain anything," Nolan says, reading my thoughts. Reading probably everyone's thoughts.

Thomas drops the sweater back into the box and folds the flaps shut.

"No, except it's obvious Julie meant something to this family, something more than any of us understands," he says, sounding angry. He stands and grabs one of the boxes. "Let's bring these downstairs."

I raise myself up and follow, closing a box and pushing it with my foot until it falls through the opening and crash-lands in the room below. Thomas leaves the attic first, followed by Allison, Eli, Kayla, and Nolan. When only Forrester and I remain, he looks at me with a face exhausted — but eyes alight with determination.

"I need to find out who she is," he says as I prepare to head down the ladder.

I nod and lower myself onto the upper rungs.

I understand his desire.

I need to find out who the hell she is, too.

THOMAS

UNDER THE DOCK, HALFWAY under the water, my world split between the quiet deep and the hushed voices still harsh against the natural mellow of the day.

"We could go west. Start close to home. We won't go far. But …"

"She's worse now, Simon. We can't … this won't help."

"It *will*. We'll be prepared. We'll make arrangements for assistance, and we'll map out everything before we leave."

"But why now? Why not years ago, when it would have been easier?"

"Why do we wait for anything, Oscar? We don't want to bother with the inconvenience — we're afraid of what will go wrong — we think we have infinite time to spare. She almost died last month. They said it could happen again. We don't have time to waste. We never have time to waste."

NOLAN

Me: Any news?

B: NO. Out with parents for a late lunch.

Me: Fuck. Okay, I'll check back later …

Whatcha eating?

B: :) I knew you couldn't resist. Burgers. What's on your menu for dinner tonight?

Me: A full-fledged Thanksgiving feast, apparently.

My cousin promises she has culinary skills.

We'll see if she's right.

B: Sounds delicious/potentially lethal.

I smirk at my phone, tempted to respond to Brandon's latest

message but knowing if I do I'll risk getting caught. Not that I think anyone would even notice. They're all too invested in the sweater we found in the attic.

I'm not sure why it's such a big deal, but I'd be lying if I didn't fess up to being creeped out by it. Maybe it's the screaming, whatever that means. That, and the way my brother — not to mention Kayla and Hailey — looked ghastly when he pulled the sweater from the box.

Who knew knitted wool could be so terrifying?

I put away my phone and help gather the stuff we threw into the guest room and take it down to the main floor, laying it out to be packed in Forrester's car tomorrow. We bring the boxes with Julie's clothes, too, but not to pack up. These we're heaping onto the junk trailer. Whoever Julie is and regardless of the original purpose for placing the clothes in the attic, they've been there for ages. They're also worn, so badly worn they're not even acceptable for donation or costuming.

Forrester keeps the polished wooden box Hailey says is probably full of old jewelry. Eli suggests smashing it to see if there's anything valuable inside, but Forrester says he'll take it home and pick the lock when he's got more time. Thomas takes the pink teddy bear from one of the boxes, too. I guess he figures if ever she were to want something from the attic stash, the teddy bear would be it.

"Do you want to look through the pictures again?" Allison asks as we stuff handfuls of clothing into a garbage bag. "See if we can find something that might give us a better idea of who she was?"

"Not now," Hailey says. "I'm hungry and sick of cleaning. Plus, I've got to get back to dinner. I think … I think we need to go over all of this shit. But later, okay? For now, let's eat. We need a rest."

"I think that's a good idea," Eli agrees. "Anyway, we'd probably have more luck asking our parents about it at home than we will looking through old pictures here."

"Not bloody likely," Thomas mumbles, crossing his arms over

his chest. "Our parents wouldn't tell us anything about the fight, so what makes you think they'd be willing to divulge information about this?"

"*Regardless*," I say, putting a hand on my brother's shoulder, "I think Hailey's right about taking a break." I give Thomas an earnest look he's instantly suspicious of. "You owe us dessert, after all," I remind him with a smile.

"Oh, I get it. You just want to put off our search so you can watch me embarrass myself, is that it?" he asks. He tries to be angry, but a grin still cracks through at the sight of my evil gleam.

"Precisely," I say, pushing him toward the kitchen.

Thomas sighs, twisting one of his gauges as he approaches the scuffed counter. I have no actual desire to eat a pie baked by my brother, and I know he doesn't think a break is the best idea right now. But as eerie and riveting as this strange mystery is, it's not the goal of the weekend to hunt the ghosts of old girlfriends or whatever the hell else it is we're aimlessly chasing. Half of our group wants to investigate. But the other half — with me included — wants to push through this weekend without any major time delays, so we can go home and deal with more pressing matters.

Like boyfriends and secrets and tests I'm desperate — and unprepared — to hear the result of.

I take a deep breath, fingers clutching my phone but not pulling it from my pocket. Instead, I focus on my brother, watching as he joins Hailey in the kitchen and grabs an actual can of pureed pumpkin.

"You're using the oven, you know," he tells Hailey after staring at the can for a dazed moment.

She's clanging through the cupboards looking for a suitable pot to cook the potatoes in, but she pauses to glance back at him, both eyebrows raised high.

"Yeah, I know," she says before returning to her task.

"Well, I have to cook my pie in the oven, and you're using it.

I can't bake my pie if your stupid turkey is in the oven. And we can't *eat* the pie if I can't bake it. So, *basically*, Hailey, you're ruining Thanksgiving."

She struggles to keep a straight face as she stands with a deep pot clutched in her hands. But she starts laughing before she gets a single word out.

"You're such a tool," she says, the noise stuck between a giggle and a groan. "Why don't you make the pie now, and when the turkey's done, you can use the oven. That way, dessert will be fresh and hot when dinner is over."

His stare is once again suspicious as he swivels back to his can.

"I suppose that *might* work," he admits.

She shakes her head, filling the pot with water as Thomas searches for a can opener.

I twist away from the group, walking over to the wide windows overlooking the bay. Pretending to admire the beauty of nature, I fish out my phone and send Brandon another quick message.

Me: Thomas is baking a pie.

B: NO. You're getting it on camera, right???

Me: If only. I'm not supposed to have my phone on me, remember?

B: Not fair. This is one disaster I'd love to witness.

Me: I promise I'll give you a detailed re-enactment.

> B: Okay. Also, maybe promise me you
> won't eat any of it.

> Me: Probably a wise decision.

"Where's the pie crust?" Thomas asks, not more than two minutes after opening the can of pumpkin.

I twist back around to see Hailey standing beside her pot, one hand on her hip, the other shaking salt into the water.

"We didn't buy a pie crust," she says, keeping her back to him. "You have to *make* the crust."

"What?" Thomas slumps against the counter, scrutinizing the can. "It doesn't have a recipe for that."

"You haven't even made the crust yet?" Eli asks, sounding far more annoyed than Hailey. He sidles into the kitchen, brushing hair out of his eyes. "You know a good pastry crust takes a while to chill, right?"

"Nope, had no idea." Thomas grins, his tone cheerful even though I can see the panic in his eyes. I bet he's wishing hard he'd thought to buy a crust. Or given up all hope and bought a store-baked pie. I'm positive pumpkin-flavored cookies would have been sufficient by this point.

Eli sighs. "We're talking at least an hour for a quality crust," he grumbles as he steps up to my brother and takes the can from his grasp.

"Well, it doesn't need to be quality. Just … edible, right?" Thomas asks.

The look Eli gives him rivals any of Thomas's most angsty expressions, the ones he doesn't frequent these days but that, a few years ago, made regular visits to his face. For the first time, I see a family resemblance between the two.

"No, not right," Eli snaps. He nudges Thomas away from the counter and pulls a pair of black, plastic-rimmed glasses from the pocket of his plaid overshirt. "I'll make the damn pie. But it won't be ready for a couple of hours yet. Dinner will be long over."

"Whatever," Kayla says from the oak dinner table. "It'll be a late-night snack."

"Sounds good to me," Thomas adds, stepping back to let Eli take the reins.

Hailey stares at Eli with something close to shock, but as my brother passes by her — his eyebrows raised in surprise — she smirks.

"You stay," she says, grabbing his arm before he can escape back to the living room. "If you're not making dessert, you can carve the turkey. You're the head of this household, after all."

"Am I?"

"Well, you're the oldest. That's close enough." She shrugs.

She says it all with casual ease, but even from across the living room I can tell the effect on Thomas is weird. I know my brother well, and he doesn't buy the idea he'll ever find the "right" person and decide to settle down. He told me once that all girls are the "right" girl for him — it's all a matter of the right time, right place, right feeling. He likes the infinite possibilities of all the beautiful women he's yet to meet, and while I think his views are depressing (and occasionally gross), I'm certain they're not the ramblings of a lonely guy trying to pretend he doesn't need someone in his life. Thomas has an insatiable thirst for adventure. His yearning for discovery extends to continuously meeting new people, too.

Family's important, and I think he understands that. But head of the household is not something I ever expect he'll be in any situation other than this.

Still, he must decide to enjoy the moment while it lasts, as he sets about getting the turkey out of the oven with a proud smile on his face.

With an ache in my chest I sigh, turning back to the window so I can tell Brandon that the near catastrophic dessert situation has been (disappointingly) averted. Then I return to the kitchen before anyone suspects what I'm doing.

I've got to give it to Hailey. The turkey is cooked, its skin brown and crisp, the wafting aroma as Thomas sets it on the stovetop drawing the rest of us like moths. We crowd around the table and the counters, breathing deep and smiling.

"After dinner's over, we can go down to the basement," Forrester says as Thomas hunts through the drawers for something to carve with. "The TV's still down there. There's no cable or anything, but we could watch a movie."

"I want s'mores," Hailey says from overtop the stuffing pot.

"I thought you wanted pie," Eli says as he takes the dough he's formed into a cling-wrapped ball and puts it in the fridge. I'm impressed with his skills. I'm even more impressed the pantry had the ingredients necessary for pastry.

"Thomas wants pie. *I* want s'mores," Hailey corrects.

"Hate to tell you, there won't be time for s'mores," Allison says. "Rain's coming. A whole storm. It'll be here by the time dinner's over."

"Well, dinner's about to start, so it'll have to hurry up," Thomas smiles, slicing into the meat. The knife cuts smooth. The turkey looks delicious.

While Thomas slices, I help to set the table. We pile plates and utensils next to potatoes and stuffing and green beans. Hailey mixes the gravy and sets it out in a handmade purple coffee mug. Thomas heaps slices of turkey onto a plate and brings it to the table once everyone's picked their beverage of choice and has settled down, ready to eat.

We're eager, all seven of us, for the first time this whole day. I don't know what the others are thinking, but I'm starving, and before us is a perfect Thanksgiving table complete with mismatched plates and hungry expressions all around.

Thomas begins dishing out the turkey. And then we eat and drink and talk until we can all barely move.

Somewhere between my first and third helpings, the rain begins.

When dinner is over, I check my phone to find five missed messages from Brandon.

B: The test has been taken.
   The results are in.

B: Positive.

B: You're not here, but I know exactly
   how you'll react. You'll mutter "shit,
   shit, shit" like it's a mantra, and then
   you'll ask me if I'm really, truly sure.
   So, I'll save you the trouble. I'm sure.
   It's positive. Pregnant.

B: And before you ask, no. I don't have
   a fucking clue what we're supposed
   to do now.

HAILEY

AN UNQUESTIONABLE ADVANTAGE TO cooking is not having to clean up afterwards. Once the meal is finished, I leave the others to scrape gravy off plates and scrounge for containers to store the leftovers in while I go upstairs to brush my teeth. I don't intend to stay up for long. I'm not one for being alone in places thick with shadows like this. But once my teeth are fresh, I can't manage to pass all the dark doorways on my way back without first veering through one of them.

Simon's room is ordinary. The teal paint is old, and there are a few spots where dirt has left a permanent smudge on the white plastic light switch and the frame surrounding the door. But the bed is made, the brown satin comforter rustling beneath my weight as I settle into a cross-legged position at its foot. Inside, it's easy to spot the scratch on the dresser and the streaks on the mirror above it. An empty nail sticks out of the wall where a picture used to hang, and the brown curtains framing the dark window are frayed.

The room is simple, the decor cheap and boring. But it doesn't feel like the room of a dead man.

I'm curious to know if Forrester had a creeping chill when he tidied in here earlier. The air is warm and fresh now, and I'm not uneasy sitting on my late uncle's bed. I'm not even sad. Either there's something wrong with me or cheesy movies overplay the emotions of estranged relatives.

I'm annoyed our family stopped talking. I want to know who the hell Julie is and why Simon's stored her old clothes in the attic. And I'm bothered by the *idea* of my uncle being dead. But the sadness doesn't make my bones ache. The squeeze on my lungs only comes when I think about Forrester, when I picture my cousin dealing with all of this shit on his own. My uncle's newly acquired non-existence doesn't rattle my nerves. His death is only an unpleasant and unhappy fact of life.

"Hey." I swivel my head around to see Allison leaning against the doorframe, her hands tucked into the pockets of her pants. "Kitchen's clean. We're going to head down to the basement now."

I nod, but I don't move from the bed — and she stays still in the doorway.

"I only have one memory of Uncle Simon," I say after a moment. I'm not sure why I've been struck with the sudden need to start rambling about the past. Maybe it's a continuation of the talk Allison and I had when we cleaned the guest room this morning. Or maybe it's because I've been rambling about the past in some form or another all day. "I think that's kind of pathetic. I mean, I remember him being around. I have family memories with him included, but only one that's just about him."

"That's more than I have," Allison admits, and I nod again as if that's the kind of response I was expecting. "Is it a good one?"

"I'm not sure." I shrug. "It was my eighth birthday. He bought me a present. A pair of earrings. They were beaded, and I think they might have been triangles or … I don't know, tents or something. I didn't get a great look because my mother got pissed and snatched them away so quick you would've thought he'd bought me porn. So, I guess it wasn't that great. I remember my mother saying 'How dare you' and Aunt Shirley muttering 'I told you' under her breath. But I also remember Uncle Simon looking at me when they both started bitching. He was sorry. Genuinely sorry I didn't get to keep the gift he bought me. I thought that part was nice."

"Not tents," Allison says, her voice cutting through the image of my uncle's face drawn in a silent apology.

"What?"

"The earrings," Allison clarifies. "They weren't tents. They were teepees."

"How do you …" I stop asking how she knows what those earrings looked like when I remember she was there, sitting on one side of me while Kayla sat on the other, like it always was when we were kids and we were a family. The *how* of her knowledge isn't important, anyway. Not as important as the *what*. "Teepees?" I mutter, thinking back to the vague memory and trying in vain to picture the dangling beads.

"Yeah," Allison says. "Orange and brown and white teepees. They were cute. I thought it was so weird when your mom took them away."

"Fucking hell," I breathe, the words a sigh I've uttered a thousand times before. "No shit my mother flipped."

"She's really against all that Native stuff, isn't she?" Allison asks.

I finger the feather around my neck, ignoring Allison's choice of word as I work to keep old anger at bay.

"Unbelievably so," I say, pushing down the rage and the tingling remnants of confusion I can't quash even after all these years.

"But why?" Allison asks.

I wish the answer was as simple as the question.

"She has her reasons," I say, "but I don't know what they are. I speculate, and I'm sure some of my guesses are true. But I don't know a damned thing for certain." I look up at my cousin and fail to smile. "Worst part is, I think I might be too chickenshit to find out."

"What do you mean?"

She steps into the room and takes up a new post leaning against the wall beside the door. She looks so much like her brother. If she chopped off her hair, it'd be impossible to tell them apart.

"I've kept in touch with the leaders from the camp I attended over the summer. One of them is a part-time professor at Trent University, and she has a connection with a reservation up north," I tell her. "There's an open invitation for me to spend time up there. A few days, a few weeks ... however long I want. I can immerse myself in the culture, see what living there is like. When she offered the opportunity, I thought it was my chance to piece together the story of my mother's life. But every time I go to email her about setting something up for next summer, I'm too fucking terrified to go through with it."

Allison smirks. The expression's unexpected, but I'm dazzled by its ease.

"I never took you for the kind of girl who let fear change her plans," she says. She scratches at a pimple on her neck, the motion automatic. "I don't know you well anymore. But the Hailey I *used* to know ... she would have jumped at the chance to get her answers."

"You think?" I say, flipping one pigtail over my shoulder and loving the way the dark strands I once despised now glisten in the artificial glow of the bedroom light. "I never cared about knowing all the answers. I never wanted to be the kind of girl who changed the world."

"Really?" Allison laughs in surprise. "That's all I've ever dreamt about. If not changing it, at least leaving my mark."

"You'd go to the reservation in an instant, wouldn't you?" I ask.

Allison smiles, her eyes bright in a way I haven't seen all weekend.

"Damn straight I would," she says. "Especially if there was something to discover."

"Even if the discovery might be horrendous?"

Allison falters for half a second, her lips dropping to a gentler curve. "Answers are answers. Sometimes they're not what we want to hear, but knowing is better."

"I'm not so sure," I mumble, looking down at my necklace as I stroke the feather. "I always liked the idea of living an ordinary life. I thought I'd grow up, get a job, work the week and play the weekend away. Ordinary — and nice."

"So, what changed?"

I look back at Allison and lick my lips.

"I realized why my mother didn't talk about her old life," I say. "Bad things must have happened, and because of that she refuses to share any of her upbringing. The bad or the good. Because I can't believe there was *no* good. Not when we both search for *Mahkan Atchakos* and she tells me stories about the origins of dogs and wolves."

Allison doesn't interrupt to ask for clarification, and I don't bother to translate the name my mother doesn't use, the one I only learned a month ago. The terminology is not of significance right now. The hard truth of what I'm admitting is.

"The more she refused to talk, the angrier I got, until the anger turned to desperation," I explain. "I figured if things were that bad, something needed to be done about it. So, I started a mental crusade. I mapped out my life, decided I would earn my degree and go up north to fix the problems she faced. But the more I researched, the more unsettling the facts became. Imagining the truth and knowing it aren't the same. Turns out, I'm not sure I'm ready to delve into my mother's life. Not when she's worked so damned hard to keep me away from it. I'm not sure I'm capable of making a difference to a problem so huge."

"You can try," Allison says, pushing off from the wall. "And that's a hell of a lot more than our parents ever did. It's more than Eli does now. It's more than Nathan does, too."

Now it's my turn to smirk. "Is that why you don't want him around? He doesn't try hard enough for your satisfaction?"

Allison rolls her eyes. "Nathan doesn't try hard enough for any-one's satisfaction. It's like he lacks the ability. He has no dreams, no plans, no goals. He stays attached to my hip because it's easier for him to hang around than try someone new."

"Why don't you cut him off? Eli seems to think you're keeping him enticed."

I've had my share of clingy boyfriends in the past, and in my younger days I played the clingy role myself at least once. Navigating that sort of shipwreck is not easy if you're determined to make it away free. But it's usually for the best, and I can't believe a girl as unsentimental as Allison wouldn't agree.

My cousin's smirk has returned.

"If he wants to break from me, all he has to do is try," she says, her voice smoky and low.

I laugh as I get off the bed, my chuckle girlish next to Allison's sexy purr. I smooth the comforter and follow her out to the hallway. After I switch off the lights, I survey the darkness, remembering the earrings my uncle bought me a long time ago.

"Simon tried," I say with a sharp twitch of what might be actual grief. "He tried to connect me to my heritage, in whatever small way he could. That was great of him." I look at Allison and put an arm around her waist as we head back downstairs. "That was really fucking great."

KAYLA

I HATE THE BASEMENT at my house. Always have. When I was a child, it was a dungeon of perpetual darkness, the place where bogeymen and ghouls resided. My brother liked to tell me stories of the countless scores of people he swore had been hacked at, burned alive, and otherwise murdered in our home. I believed all his gruesome tales, and to think of them now, it's amazing I was ever bothered by Forrester's lie about the shed outside. Night dwellers, even vampires, are far less frightening than the blood-soaked corpses I used to be certain were stacked in my basement.

But the cottage's lowest level has forever been a safe haven. As kids, we gathered here to play board games, watch movies, and fall asleep in comfort and company. Now, each creaking step down overwhelms me with small details I never used to notice, like the unexplained splotch of baby blue paint on the otherwise brown-beige wall, or the illogical way I get warmer as I move deeper beneath the earth.

"Nothing here has changed, has it?" Eli remarks as we reach the bottom of the stairs. His gaze is full of the distaste he's worn all day, but his tone reveals a note of tenderness I don't believe he'd ever stoop to fake. First the abandoned fort in the shed, and now this? I think even Eli's succumbing to the charm of this place. And why shouldn't he? We had a lot of good times in this brown-shaded and musty-scented room.

I wonder if it holds any of the same magic for Forrester. He's had a full decade to create a set of memories the rest of us never had the chance to build. Do his feet still tingle when he squishes his toes into the too old but still soft flooring? Or is this just another room, another place he has to give away because his dad has died?

"Dad never bothered with upgrading to a DVD player," Forrester says, dragging a large cardboard box from the closet on the far side of the room. "And there's no network connection, so we can't stream anything. We've got a VCR, though. Thing's ancient, but amazingly, it still works."

I step off the stairs, my eyes traveling to the nearby fireplace and the space over the mantel above it. A painting is hung there, one I'm sure has been around for years, but one I've never bothered to look at before. Yellow, orange, and muted green foliage surrounds a white-barked tree shedding its few remaining leaves. This painting is not the same as the one we have at home. Different style, different hand. But although I'm not familiar with the painting itself, I'm sure the work is from another Group of Seven artist.

The painting hangs crooked on the wall, and I wrap my arms around myself as I flop onto the old sofa, the warmth of the picture and its off-kilter resting place making me shiver.

"What do we want to watch?" Forrester asks.

Hailey grins, dropping to her knees beside the box and rummaging through it. I see the worn covers of dozens of VHS tapes, big and bulky compared to the slim cases of the few Blu-rays we still have at home. For a few seconds, the movies seem fake, their thick shapes less like films than like a weird collection of dusty old books. But then I remember the way we used to hunt through similar boxes when we were kids, how seemingly prehistoric the movies were even then.

"That greatly depends on what's inside." She smiles.

"There's nothing new," Forrester warns, sitting back and surveying her.

Forrester was quieter at dinner than he's been all day. While we shoved food in our mouths and prattled non-stop until the feast was complete and the dishes were washed, he remained silent and still, observing us all but not partaking in our easy conversation. I think he wanted to talk more about the sweater we found in the attic. But I'm glad he's content to have a break now. Today's been stressful in many more ways than one. We all need to surrender ourselves to the pure joy of hunting through old movie tapes to try and find the most entertaining thing to watch.

Nolan frowns when Hailey pulls out a movie without any cover at all. The plastic label on its front is so faded it's impossible to tell what the title is.

"If I know one thing about VHS, it's that we're going to be really annoyed when we have to rewind whatever we choose to play, right?" he asks.

"That's part of the magic," I say in a dreamy voice, at once saddened and amused by the fact Nolan doesn't remember watching any of these tapes with us.

He lets out a soft breath of laughter.

"This stuff is great!" Hailey exclaims from overtop of the box.

She grabs a few movies and places them on the ground, tossing others back in while she sifts through the mound of choices.

I perk up when I see a cover I recognize. "Oh! We could watch *The Notebook*!"

"*No*," Hailey says, giving me a thumbs-down.

I appeal to my other cousins, but it's a useless endeavor. All five of them take Hailey's side, leaving me to mope on the couch with glowering eyes.

Watching a romance would be weird here, anyway. The last time I saw *The Notebook* was with Hudson. He says he doesn't mind sitting through it because it puts me in a *mood*. I smile at the thought. Then my stomach tightens, and I remember this is the night we could have been in a *mood* together, the only night for who knows how many more weeks. We haven't talked much since Tuesday, since I told him of the change in our plans. We've sacrificed more than a couple of days already, and I'm scared this is how it starts — how relationships begin to end.

"Find anything *good* to watch?" Allison asks, pulling me back to the cottage and the family I chose to be with tonight.

Hailey nods without looking up.

"Tons," she sighs. "It's a matter of deciding which one to experience again."

"Hailey, you're pathetic," Thomas scolds, sitting down beside her. "These movies are awful!"

He holds up some cheap cartoon we probably watched as kids. I don't remember it in the slightest.

"There is gold here, Thomas," Hailey replies as she lifts another tape, the title covered by her fingers. "But you have to be willing to see it."

"This is going to lead to the worst movie-watching experience of my life," Eli moans.

Allison hits him with one of the sofa's raggedy red throw pillows.

The Notebook would have been nice, but I don't care what we watch. I don't even care if we watch anything at all. As Hailey and Thomas fight over what movie to put on, I go back to studying the basement's beige walls and brown carpet, the seeming unattractiveness of the room somehow making it more brilliant than any stylish decorations could. When my gaze again lands on the painting over the fireplace, it lingers until the others make their decision.

"Okay, I think we'll watch this," Hailey says at last.

I tear my eyes away from the picture to see her holding up a VHS of an old movie called *The Peanut Butter Solution*.

I smile, the bizarre movie about a kid who loses his hair and uses a concoction with peanut butter to grow it back an old favorite. I used to think this was the weirdest movie ever made, and I don't even know how a copy ended up in the cottage basement. Forrester's parents must have bought it at a garage sale or something, part of a collection of unwanted movies given a new home in this beautiful place.

Forrester gets a small fire going, and Thomas turns off the lights as Hailey pushes the tape into the VCR. She curses when she realizes she does, in fact, have to rewind it.

"Useless technology," Eli says with a shake of his head. "No wonder it's extinct."

Allison rolls her eyes, and I tuck my knees under me, my muscles tight with anticipation.

Maybe it's sad, us being stuck in a childlike state of companionship. But perhaps this is the way we break through the tangled years of distance and grab hold of one another again.

And maybe I'm reading too much into all of this. Maybe we're just watching a movie, and I'm the only one whose heart pounds as if all these tiny moments will amount to something bigger.

Hailey starts the movie from the beginning of the tape, and then she sits beside me on the couch. We curl into each other, and Allison drapes a blanket over our knees even though the room is already warm.

"This movie used to scare me," Hailey confesses as we watch the opening credits. "When I was really young. My parents were all about keeping everything happy and innocent in my childhood. If they'd even known what we were watching ..."

She laughs, the tremble of movement vibrating against my side.

"It's not so bad, having parents who want to shield you." Eli shrugs.

"Not realistic, though, is it?" Hailey says, sounding annoyed. "They keep you sheltered, and you never get to see what the world looks like. Pain, death, all that shit. You stay sheltered, and then when you do encounter it, it's way worse because you don't understand what the hell is going on. You're not prepared to be afraid or hurt or dissatisfied."

"Yeah, but sometimes it can be taken too far in the opposite direction," Allison replies. Her voice sounds hollow, like Eli's. "They make you experience the hurt and the shame. They expect you to understand all of it, and they use it against you to make their lives easier."

I raise my head from Hailey's shoulder and glance at the twins.

"What are you talking about?" I ask.

They both shake their heads, their expressions clouded.

"Family stuff," Eli mutters.

"It's personal," Allison agrees. "We shouldn't have said anything."

"But you did," Thomas chimes in. "And people don't let information like that slip when they don't want to discuss it."

Hailey chuckles beneath her breath. She must share Thomas's opinion.

"Yeah, well, we don't," Eli snaps.

Thomas looks like he wants to argue the point, and I wish he would. Whatever's happening between Eli and Allison is starting to get on my nerves. They've been arguing all day, and this of any day seems the most inappropriate for pointless disagreement. And if it's not pointless, they should talk about it with us. Because if anything's clear, it's that they are not handling the issue well on their own.

Thomas doesn't say anything else, though. He doesn't have the chance. Before he can respond to Eli, Forrester comments on the movie as if he's oblivious to the fight brewing a few seats away.

"Anyone else ever wonder what he saw in that house?" he asks, pointing to the screen as the main character enters a house after a fatal fire — the visit that terrifies him so much he goes bald.

Forrester's voice is gentle, and it dissolves any will the rest of us had to fight. I force myself to look away from the twins. Nestling back against Hailey, I focus on the movie instead.

"I always assumed it was ghosts," I say, trying to keep my voice light.

"I always thought it was corpses," Thomas replies. He laughs.

"They probably didn't leave dead bodies lying around, but it explained why he was scared so bad."

"I figured there was part of a body left. Like an arm or something. I imagined a rat gnawing on the charred meat."

Hailey says this in the most gruesome voice I think she could manage, and Thomas laughs again.

"I don't think you had to worry about your parents being over-protective," he says. "That is *not* the assumption of a shielded little girl."

"This is supposed to be a kid's movie, right?" Nolan asks, watching the movie like he's never seen it before. I wonder if he remembers any of it from when he was a kid. He would have been no more than six when we last watched it here.

I always found it amusing how he and Thomas made up the bookends of our childhood group. Nolan just made the cut-off, young but a touch too old to play with Marissa or Liam. Sometimes, his age made a big difference as a kid. Now, it's hardly noticeable. In ten more years, I doubt it'll make any difference at all.

No one addresses the twins again. We watch the movie, and soon we're involved in the story. Halfway through the running time, Eli goes upstairs to make the rest of his pie. While the movie's paused, everyone takes turns getting ready for bed, and Hailey and I rummage through the second-floor linen closet to find sheets and pillows for the pullout couch. We come back together without any lingering tension. We finish the movie, and when it's over, Eli gets the pie out of the oven while we unfold the sofa bed.

"All right," Eli says, coming down the stairs with the pie, a can of whipped cream, and seven forks. "You'd better appreciate my efforts. I'm not in the habit of baking in public."

"You're my hero," Thomas says, taking the pie and inhaling the scent I can smell even from across the room. I don't have pumpkin pie often, and I already ate a ton at dinner. Still, my stomach growls when its aroma reaches me.

We make the bed, put on some old sorority slasher, and gather together on the pullout couch. Thomas sits in the middle, and somehow all of us manage to crowd together on either side. We pass the hot, spiced pie between us, delighting in the smooth texture and flaky crust, the whipped cream melting against the warm pumpkin. Eli's an amazing baker. I don't know why he'd ever hide such a delicious talent.

Before long I'm full, comfortable, and sleepy. Over the course of the slasher movie and the small-town drama Allison puts on next, we spread out — Thomas atop the sofa cushions laid out on the floor like a cot, Forrester wrapped in a blanket on the carpet before the fireplace. The rest of us stay on the bed, no one minding the close quarters, no one feeling weird or cramped.

I don't know how many movies we put on. I make it about twenty minutes into the third film before I fall asleep.

ELI

At least
they like the pie. Damn well better. I've been working
on that pastry recipe
for a year now.

Ali once suggested I become a chef. What a laugh. I can only
    imagine
what I'd look like, covered in food,
catering to the general public's needs.

I'm glad they like it, though.
I've never made pumpkin before. My specialty's
lemon meringue.

Weirder than the pumpkin
is the fact I'm enjoying myself.
Movies, food, a roaring fire,
the rain inaudible down here.

We're in a cave,
tucked away
from the rest of the world.

It's nicer than I would have expected.
But it's only
temporary.

This cottage is outdated. It could be so much better. It has
   the potential
to be so much more.
It's not preservation of the past here.
It's laziness,
a lack of money,
a lack of sense.
This place could be magnificent.
Instead it's living inside a pathetically packed time capsule.

We go home tomorrow.
Dad will pick up Ali
because he wants
her help.

I'll leave by myself,
and I won't look back.
No lingering glances,
no feelings
of sadness
that this time in our life is over.

Forrester deserves my pity.
Our family history does not.

I'll enjoy the last hours, if I can.
I'll allow myself that much.

But after tomorrow,
this memory will fade,
and life will move on,
like it's supposed to.

ALLISON

The storm is moving in. I can hear it upstairs, and I wish we were sleeping up there so I could watch it, too. Everyone's fallen asleep around me. The fire's dead, the TV's off, and all I hear is breathing. And snoring. Thomas and Hailey both snore. Nolan's quiet but fidgety. Kayla and Forrester sleep like they're dead. And Eli, well ... I already know how my twin sleeps. Straight, unmoving, and always one feather-stroke away from jumping to attention.

Today wasn't as bad as my dream led me to believe it might be. I'm glad I don't see these people every day. The girls are irritating — Kayla meek, Hailey coarse, and each obsessed with their appearances, in one way or the other. What would either of them say if they knew I haven't given my reflection more than a cursory glance in over a year?

They'd probably tie me down and try to force me to endure a makeover.

I shudder to envision the outcome.

The boys aren't much better. Thomas is too lighthearted, and Forrester is too grave. And Nolan, well ... I've got enough skulking to deal with from Eli.

I'm not being totally fair, though. Kayla's disposition is sweet, and Hailey's got confidence I could only dream of. Thomas sees brightness in every situation, Forrester's attempt to keep hold of his senses is admirable, and Nolan's doing a much better job of hiding the reason his face flits through emotions each time he not-so-secretly checks his phone than Eli is at keeping his temper down. Anyway, I'm jealous of how easy Thomas and his brother are together.

Eli's furious with me, which is becoming a more frequent occurrence these days. I don't see the world the same way he does, but I don't want that to tear us apart. Then again, maybe losing each other is inevitable. Look at Dad and his brothers. Maybe the Hacher family is doomed to be estranged.

I want to snuggle against Kayla and fall asleep. I want to sleep so deep I don't remember any of my problems when I wake.

But it looks like I'm the only one unsettled enough to stay up for now. At least the roll of thunder above us is a comfort.

I wish I could be out of this calm and up in the storm. A storm's where I'm headed, anyway. Might as well get an early start.

KAYLA

I DON'T REMEMBER WHAT I dream about. Hudson, maybe. Or Uncle Simon. Perhaps even Julie, whoever she is. The dream is murky before I've regained consciousness, and it's gone the moment I wake with cheeks wet with tears.

I wipe the moisture away like they're droplets of stupidity. My body's shaking, and my stomach is sick. Too much food — too much pie. I try to take a deep breath and surprise myself by sobbing instead. Whatever I dreamed about, its clutch hasn't yet loosened. My lips are trembling as I chastise myself in the dark.

"Kayla?" The voice is a whisper, and it takes me a moment to locate its source on the floor. Squinting, I make out Thomas's shadow as he rises up on his elbows and rubs his eyes through a yawn. "You okay?"

"Yeah," I say, my voice at once a laugh and a sniff.

The weak tone is not enough to convince him. He crawls over to the bed, his brows furrowed. Around us bodies rise and fall in the rhythm of sleep. I don't want to wake anyone else because of my nuisance of a dream, whatever it was. Sitting up, I wonder if I can lift myself over Allison without disturbing her, until I realize Allison is not beside me. I look around the room, but it's too dark to see much of anything. She probably moved closer to Eli, more comfortable next to her brother than the cousin she doesn't know.

I slide off the bed, blinking away the sticky, sleep-filled tears. Thomas stands, grabbing my hand as he beckons for me to follow him upstairs, and I nod as he pulls me up, both of us shuffling across the carpet. Morning is still far off, and a fierce storm rages outside. Halfway up the steps, a lightning flash brightens the floor above us, thunder bellowing a few seconds behind.

When we reach the living room, I discover Allison did not move to sleep next to her twin. She's up here already, lying on the sofa and watching the storm. She glances at us as we step down into the sunken square, but then she returns her head to the sofa's arm without saying a word. Thomas doesn't seem perturbed by her presence, and I suppose I'm not, either.

We sit on the wooden step, our faces to the back windows. If it weren't for the lightning, it would be impossible to make anything out of the docks or the bay this late. But with a bright flash, the whole property blooms into view — the shadowy shed, the grassy slope, and the black water surrounded by blowing trees.

"Are you okay?" Thomas asks again once we're sitting side by side, listening to the heavy lashing of rain against the windowpanes.

This time my laugh is stronger. "Yeah. It was a stupid dream. I don't even remember what it was about. Nothing to concern yourself over."

The way he stares at me suggests he doesn't believe in stupid dreams, just as he doesn't believe in slips of the tongue. He holds my gaze, and my cheeks warm with embarrassment. I don't remember what I dreamed about or why I was crying when I woke up. But his stare is nagging, like he's trying to pull my secrets free. I'm not like the twins. I don't have some deep-buried truth I'm unwilling to reveal. My problems are, well … non-problems at a time like this.

I don't want to tell him about Hudson. Not here, with everything else going on. But Thomas doesn't stop staring, so after a lengthy pause I sigh and let the words flow.

"My boyfriend …" I shrug my shoulders and ball my hands together in my lap. "Hudson. He's away at university. He left at the end of August, and I haven't seen him since then. We talk and all, but we haven't been physically together … um, that sounded wrong. I just mean, I haven't, like, *touched* him … and that sounds even worse." I shake my head through Thomas's laugh and catch Allison's smirk from where she's listening on the sofa. "He's been away, and I haven't spent time with him in person," I clarify, my cheeks now burning hot.

"That sucks," Thomas says, the laughter almost gone from his voice. "Is that what you dreamed about? Do you miss him?"

"No," I begin, and then, "well, yes, I miss him a lot. But that's not what the dream was. I don't think so, anyway. It's just … he's coming home for Thanksgiving. Arrived yesterday, leaving Monday morning. His family is strict about celebrating with only the family. So, today … yesterday? Saturday. Saturday was the only chance we had to see each other."

"You gave it up to come here?" Thomas asks. "Kayla, you didn't have to come."

I place a hand on his arm to cut him off before he can start pitying me.

"I chose to come, and I'm not sorry I did," I explain, thinking back to the day of the funeral and the brief certainty I felt when I agreed to help. "I miss Hudson like crazy. But it's our family. It's what needed to be done."

"So why the long face?" he asks.

I smile, retrieving my hand and running it through the tangled strands of my hair. I probably look like a disaster. I didn't even wash off my makeup before bed.

"He wasn't too fond of my change of plans. He didn't see being here as something important. And now he's mad, and we're missing our chance to see each other, and I think I'm afraid this is how the end of it starts."

I blink and replay the words I've uttered out loud. Sharing so many details was definitely not part of the plan. I don't know what it is about Thomas. He grabs the truth like he's pulling silk scarves from a pocket.

"You think he'd end it because of this?" he asks.

I open my mouth to respond, but it takes a while before I figure out which words to respond with.

"No. I don't think it will be over because of this," I say at length. "But this weekend was our way to keep grasping onto one another, to keep hold of *us*. Everyone told us to break up before he went away, you know? And we told them they were wrong. And, I still think they were. I don't want to be without Hudson. But I'm afraid it's different on his end. He's away, after all. My day-to-day is the same as always, while he's in a different world. I'm afraid he'll drift. This weekend was our tether. I wanted to pull it tighter, make sure it's not going to break. Make sure his heart is still docked with mine. Instead, I've frayed an edge, and that could lead to the rope snapping somewhere down the line."

"Do you believe he loves you?" Thomas asks.

This time my response is quick.

"I know he does," I say. "That's one of the only things I'm certain of."

"Then this weekend won't hurt anything. Frayed edges can be repaired. They don't all snap."

I breathe deep, my full stomach straining with the effort.

"I know, but being oblivious to what will happen next is still tragic, isn't it?"

"I've always liked not knowing." He grins. "It's more fun that way. Surprises are around every corner, and being surprised by them is awesome."

Thunder cracks outside, and for a minute all three of us are silent. When Thomas moves his arm, my eyes travel to his black-and-sepia-inked wrist as he scratches his elbow.

"Thomas, where did you get the idea for your tattoos?" I ask.

He startles at the sound of my voice, and then looks down at his wrists, joining the two together.

"There's this painting in the hallway at home," he says. "It's right across from my bedroom, so I've looked at it pretty much every day for as long as I can remember. On my eighteenth birthday, some of my friends took me to an excellent tattoo artist. They made the appointment months before, so I couldn't disappoint them and not get something done. I spent, like, an hour thinking about it, and then I remembered the painting. I found it online, and Miranda — the tattoo artist — she freehanded this based on it. Stunning ability. Stunning woman, too."

My fingertips tingle with triumph. I knew the tattoo was from a painting.

"What painting was it?" I ask, keeping my voice light and only mildly intrigued.

I'd put money on it being painted by one of seven individuals. I think of the picture in our kitchen and the one downstairs above the fire. Five brothers, seven artists. I wonder if everyone has a painting at home.

"I don't even know what it's called." Thomas smirks, studying his wrists. "But it's by J something MacDonald. I remember that much."

"J.E.H. MacDonald." I smile, nudging him.

"Yeah, how'd you know?"

Thomas looks at me, his eyebrows raised. I shrug my shoulders and turn back to the windows.

"Just recognized the style," I murmur.

I squeeze my hands into fists and press them against my thighs as I watch the rain.

HAILEY

THE DAMN BUZZING WAKES me. Right in the middle of the night and inches from my ear like some kind of incessant bee.

"What the hell?"

I force my eyes open and wipe a disgusting slick of saliva from my chin. Charming. I hate waking up. Being awake is fine, but waking up is the worst. Only sleeping for a couple of hours doesn't help, nor does the fact I ate my weight in turkey and pie before I hit the sack in the first place.

The buzzing sounds again, the second warning of an incoming message no one seems to catch but me. The phone's light is easy to spot where it rests in Nolan's sleeping hand. I brush hair out of my eyes and maneuver the phone out from under my cousin's palm. I'm an expert at this task. With two younger siblings, I know how to recover stolen treasures after miniature thieves have passed out cold.

The screen is still lit when I move it close to my face.

> B: Can't sleep. Mind's reeling. Text me
> as soon as you're awake, okay?

The message doesn't concern me, but the phone woke me up, and that pisses me off. I hate when people text in the middle of the night. I always make a point to turn my phone off so I'm not bothered by annoying people who are usually not in their right frame of mind. My stomach sloshes and squeals, discomfort I wouldn't feel if

I was still asleep. So, screw the ethics of invading someone's phone privacy.

I slide the touch screen to open the message, only to be blocked by a passcode. I try Nolan's birthday, but the phone buzzes me away, resetting the screen for a second attempt. The number could be random, or some digits I don't know the significance of. Wouldn't be too difficult to stump me. Still, I do my best. I think of a number easy to remember, difficult for friends or strangers to guess. I try Thomas's birthday next. When the phone unlocks, I'm almost giddy with pride.

I expect to scroll through the conversation with B before going through Nolan's other contacts and seeing if there's anything worth snooping through. But the open stream of messages is enough to stop me in my tracks. Before the lament of not being able to sleep, there was an exchange of needing to talk tomorrow, of needing to be together to figure it all out. An "I love you" here, a "Love you, too" there, all typical teenaged romance stuff.

But when I slide back a little further ... the tiniest smidge further ... I figure out why B can't seem to sleep.

"Pregnant?"

I whisper the word out loud. I can't help it. This isn't the kind of message I was expecting. Not even close.

But my big mouth ruins the perfect moment of solitary awe. I hear the rustle beside me before I comprehend who's making the noise. When Nolan speaks, his voice is groggy with sleep. He sounds adorable. And young. Too young to be a father.

"Hailey?" He asks the question like he's not convinced he isn't dreaming. But when my eyes shift over to his, he recovers his alertness in record time. "What are you doing with my phone?" he asks in a much less adorable — and much more vicious — whisper.

He makes an instant grab for the phone, and I only just manage to pull back my arm.

"Pregnant?" I whisper in response, not sure what other comment to make. The word is too big. Saying it once isn't sufficient to get it off my tongue.

Nolan's eyes shift from being narrowed in anger to shooting wide with panic. He scrambles up to a sitting position, and I have to throw myself backwards to avoid his grabbing hands. I roll over the side of the pullout, banging my knee against the metal frame on my way to the ground. I stifle a curse and stagger up, my knee throbbing in pain for the second time in less than twelve hours.

"Give me my phone!" Nolan whisper-screams as I hobble over to the stairs. I'm not about to relinquish this goldmine of information, but I can't keep bouncing around the basement without waking everyone up.

Nolan trails behind me like a little kid chasing the big sister who's stolen his favorite action figure. *Little kid.* Nolan's only a little kid. He shouldn't even be *thinking* about sex.

My own accusation is idiotic. I was no stranger to sex at his age. But I never did the deed without proper precautions. I can't believe he'd be so stupid. I want to find Thomas and give him a good thump on the head. He should've taught his brother better.

Although, I guess it's not Thomas's responsibility. It should have been up to their father. But the Hacher men don't seem able to keep their shit together. The birds and the bees probably slipped my uncle's mind.

Nolan grabs my shirt as we reach the main floor. I twist away from him and dive for the living room, stepping backwards to look at his black expression as he approaches me again.

"I can't believe this, Nolan!" I say in a louder voice, phone raised above my head. "I can't believe you … you're …"

"Hailey, this is none of your business!" Nolan snaps. "Give me back my phone!"

"Woah, what's going on?"

The voice makes me jump. I face the living room again, and through the stormy darkness see Thomas, Kayla, and Allison. Allison sits up from where she's been lying across the couch, while Thomas and Kayla stand.

"Thomas," I say, addressing his question, "do you know what kind of trouble your baby brother has gotten himself into?"

I waggle the phone, while Nolan begins swearing up a storm to rival the one outside.

"Hailey, shut up, will you?" he says, rushing for me.

Thomas gets between us and holds Nolan back, looking at us both like we've gone insane.

"Seriously," he says, his voice indeed more serious than I've ever heard it. "What's going on?"

"Nothing," Nolan mutters. "Hailey took my phone."

"Wow." Thomas fixes me with an expression I can't make out in the darkness. "That's rule number one with Nolan, didn't you know? You never take his phone. *Nev-er*. I'm surprised you're still alive."

"I didn't mean to take his phone," I say, but when Nolan *growls* at me, I amend my response. "A stupid text woke me up. I wanted to see what was so important it couldn't wait until morning."

"A text?"

Nolan stops pushing against his brother. His whole body softens, and with a helpful flash of lightning I see the concern falling over his features. My stomach drops. Kid or no, he's not brushing this off like it's no big deal. Of course he's not. I should never have assumed otherwise. He's worried. He should be.

"That's it?" Thomas asks, dropping his arms as Nolan stops struggling. "You took his phone to read a text, and now you won't give it back? I didn't realize the regression had hit us so hard. I thought you were seventeen, Hailey, not seven."

I fix Thomas with a sarcastic, star-bright smile as I hand him the phone.

"See for yourself," I say.

Thomas takes the phone and stares at the now black screen like he's not quite sure what it is.

"Thomas," Nolan says.

With only a second of hesitation, Thomas hands the phone back to his brother without taking a peek. The moment is touching. Nolan is relieved, and proud of his brother for not giving in to temptation. He thinks his secret is safe. Unfortunately for him, I've always been a lousy secret-keeper.

"He's knocked someone up," I say, the words so flat they don't even sound like mine.

"He what?" Kayla asks.

Thomas turns back to me, his brow furrowed.

"You have to be mistaken," he says with confusion and amusement.

I shake my head and point to the phone now in Nolan's hand, the boy's fingers texting with a pace furious enough to match his expression.

"I'm not," I say. "Someone named B. Got her pregnant. Says so right in the message, if you'd bothered to check."

"*No*," Kayla says in pure shock.

"Bea's pregnant?" Thomas asks in a far more subdued voice. He looks back at his brother, while his brother raises his head from the screen.

"Thomas," he says, his voice gentle.

"Bea's pregnant?" his brother repeats.

"You can't be a father," Kayla says.

She seems more stunned than any of us, Thomas included.

"I'm not going to be," Nolan seethes, his eyes still trained on Thomas.

"You're not going to ignore her," I say, confused by his quick change from concerned boyfriend to careless bystander. But then it occurs to me there are other options aside from simple abandonment.

"You need to talk about your options first, Nolan. You can't make a rash decision here. This isn't something you can just throw away."

"I'm not throwing anything away!" Nolan replies, his voice rising.

"Nolan," Thomas says, and I already know what the rest of his sentence will be. "Bea's pregnant?"

"Yes," Nolan answers. He looks crestfallen. Not scared, only ... upset. "She is. She found out tonight."

"I think I need to sit down," Thomas says.

Nolan grabs his arm as Thomas begins to sway. Kayla and I rush over, while Allison stands and tells us to bring him to the couch. He sits hard and bends over so his head is touching his knees.

"Geez, you'd think he was the one having the baby," Allison mumbles.

Nolan heaves a great sigh, throwing his hands in the air like he can't take the sight of us anymore.

"That's because he is," he says. "And you've gone and told him in the least sensitive way fucking possible." These words are directed at me, and I stare at him in amazement, partially because of what he's said and partially because of the fierce way he's said it.

"Wait, I thought you were the one ...." Kayla looks at Nolan and then at me.

"No, I didn't get anyone pregnant," Nolan finishes for her.

"But the phone," I say, shaking my head. "It said pregnant. B. Thomas said B was pregnant, and you agreed."

"Bea *is* pregnant," Nolan says through clenched teeth.

"Yes, that's the point. Nolan, I read those messages. That's not the way you talk to a friend. Are you ... you're not both seeing the same girl, are you?"

The idea makes me squeamish, my earlier inclination to vomit returning.

"What? That's gross ... no." Nolan rolls his eyes and gives me a hard stare. "Bea is pregnant. B-E-A, as in Beatrice. *B*, the letter B, is short for Brandon. Beatrice's brother."

"But Hailey said you two were …," Kayla begins.

"Her brother and my boyfriend," Nolan sighs, exasperated.

Kayla's mouth drops open.

"So, you didn't get a girl pregnant … because you have a boyfriend?" she says, the words slow.

"Yes," Nolan replies.

He looks a thousand leagues beyond pissed. I can't blame him. I spilled two of his secrets in the space of about five minutes, which might be a new record for me.

But his look of pure hatred doesn't reach its uppermost limit until a few seconds later, when Kayla bursts out laughing.

"What's so funny?" Nolan snaps.

Kayla shakes her head, covering her mouth like she's trying to stop the giggles from pouring forth.

"Nothing," she breathes, lowering her eyes from his. "It's not … it's not funny at all!"

She breaks into another fit, while Allison turns away from us, a smirk on her lips.

Thomas is looking at us all like we're nuts. I try to make level eye contact with Nolan, to show him I'm serious about the issue at hand. But when I see the fire there, I can't help cracking into a grin as well. I snort, actually *snort*, and then push myself into Kayla's side, half nudging her and half burying my face in so Nolan can't see me.

The situation is not funny — in fact it's quite serious, with a little sweetness thrown into the mix. Nolan and his boyfriend must have something meaningful, the way they've been exchanging worried texts about the fate of Brandon's sister. And I'm curious to know how Thomas fits into all of this. He's petrified, that's easy enough to see. But he doesn't seem surprised to learn about Nolan's correspondence. So, maybe Nolan's boyfriend isn't a secret, after all. At least not to Thomas.

I should be consoling him. Or I should at least be continuing my tirade of bitchiness and pounding him with questions. But all of this is ludicrous, like a melodrama playing out before our eyes, terrible and fucking fantastic.

Nolan's not impressed. He kneels down before his brother.

"It can't be me, though, right?" Thomas asks, looking for answers in his baby brother's eyes. Kayla, Allison, and I work to get ourselves under control. Our manic laughter is not needed right now. "It has to be her boyfriend, doesn't it?"

Nolan shrugs.

"It might be," he says with an unconvincing smile. "She says she doesn't know. She thinks timing-wise, it could have been right before she met him. While you two were still spending time together."

"But we didn't ... I mean we weren't ... we were careful," Thomas splutters.

I haven't seen him look this unsure of himself all day. I doubt he often looks this way — terrified doesn't suit him.

"She's not sure about that, either," Nolan says, looking just as unsure and maybe even more uncomfortable. "She, uh, she missed a couple of pills or something."

"Idiot," Allison murmurs.

Thomas gives her a dark look while he runs a hand through his un-gelled strip of hair.

"Bea's not an idiot," he says, his words solid and thick.

"You miss pills, you use alternative methods of backup," Allison retorts. "Everyone knows that."

"I don't," I remark.

I don't use the pill, so maybe if I did, I'd know more about it. But I didn't learn about anything related to sex until I discovered it first-hand. If my suspicions are correct, my mother experienced some stuff too early. Her response was to never tell me a thing.

"Bea's not an idiot," Thomas says again, but he's already focused back on Nolan. He doesn't care what we think, and I'm glad.

"No," Nolan agrees, "but she *is* pregnant. And there *is* a chance it could be yours."

"Is she even going to keep it?" I ask, unable to suppress the question.

Thomas looks at me, and then back at his brother. Nolan shrugs, like he doesn't know what he's supposed to say.

"She just found out, like, a few hours ago … I don't think she's thought that far ahead."

He puts a hand on his brother's shoulder. When they look at each other, both of them serious, they're almost like twins.

"Is she planning on telling me?" Thomas asks.

The second of sameness passes, as Nolan's expression changes to one of being the bearer of awkward news.

"It's still early days," he says with a crack in his voice. "And I'm sure she knows you'll find out. She wouldn't have told Brandon if she didn't want … but she's got Rodge now, and I don't know …"

Sometimes a trail into silence says more than any spoken words. Rodge must be Bea's new boyfriend. And Bea must think she's got a future with this guy. From Nolan's look, and the dark glint in Thomas's eyes, I'm guessing they both understand Bea's top priority is to keep things going with the guy she hopes is the father — not to break it apart by running to the friend she hopes is not.

"Well, then, that's it," Thomas says. A hint of remorse flits between the words, but then he blinks and sits up straight. "There's nothing more to be said about it."

"Thomas, that's not …"

Nolan tries to bring him back into the discussion, but his effort is useless. Thomas is reclining against the cushions now, his eyes staring up at the windows in the high ceiling as his fingers stray up to fiddle with his ear.

"Some storm out there, eh?" he says, his arms crossed over his chest.

I look around, trying to decide which of us girls is going to answer him. But the voice to respond is deeper, softer.

"It always seems wild through all these windows," Forrester replies.

I turn, along with everyone else, to look at the top of the staircase leading down into the basement. Forrester and Eli are standing on the main floor before the stairwell. I'm not sure how long they've been there or how much they've heard.

"I remember being scared witless one year," Forrester continues. "Thought for sure a tree was going to crash through the roof."

"I can imagine." Thomas smiles.

The last two members of our group walk into the living room. Kayla offers Nolan a sympathetic glance before he slumps down onto the floor and begins texting again. Then Allison speaks up, talking about storms, about the worst one she remembers. The topic turns into a game, each of us recalling the harshest of stormy days and nights, times when the sky turned green or hail rained down like gigantic wooden blocks falling over our homes.

Nolan doesn't join us, but he does put his phone away after a few minutes. He watches his brother, and I watch him, none of us speaking about the life-altering news we just discovered.

We're so ill-equipped to handle this shit. Each and every one of us. All we know how to do is sweep the pain away and pretend we're fine. But sooner or later it's going to come back.

I'd like to know what the hell will happen then.

NOLAN

Me: So much for being tactful. Thomas knows about Bea.

B: Did you tell him??

Me: No. My stupid cousin Hailey stole my phone while I was sleeping.

B: Wtf? She told him?

Me: Sort of. She actually told him I got Bea pregnant.

B: …

Me: She thought you were the one taking the test. She told Thomas "B" was pregnant. He figured it out.

B: Okay, I know this is serious, but I literally lol'd at that.

Me: It is pretty ridiculous. You
should've seen it.

I felt like I was in some bad
after-school special.

B: Cousins are as bad as siblings, aren't
they?

Me: I think in my case, they're
much worse.

B: Speaking of … what's he going to
do now?

Me: I don't know.

B: It's a lot to take in. Bea's going
crazy.

But she told Rodge. She's staying at
his tonight.

He seemed to take it okay. I think he
wants to help.

Me: Good. With everyone's
luck, it's his, anyway.

B: And if it's not?

Me: I have no idea.

B: I miss you.

Me: I miss you, too. A few more
hours and I'll be on my way
home.

B: Be on your way to me instead, okay?

Me: That's what I meant. Home,
you … it's the same thing.

The morning is cold when I step outside. The sun has only just made an appearance, peeking out between the trees on the far side of the bay. Without its warmth, I'm surrounded by air crisp and damp, the earth soggy from the storm that passed sometime around four in the morning.

We fell asleep in the living room, all of us sprawled on the floor and furniture. I tossed and turned for a while, but I must have dozed off at some point because I was surprised when Thomas shook me awake, beckoning me to follow him and Forrester outside. Neither of them looked like they'd slept at all. Thomas had good reason for suffering through a restless night. All things considered, it'd be stupid not to admit that Forrester did, too.

Now, Forrester hands us jackets smelling of dirt and old sweat, but I shrink into the warmth of the heavy fleece as we unload the canoe and get out the paddles. We don't say anything as we carry the boat down to the docks and lower it into the water. I'm not entirely sure why they've even included me in this venture, but I don't ask. I'm tired, and feeling bad for Thomas. Plus, I'm flattered they wanted me to join them, while the others are all still asleep inside.

A hovering mist shadows the bay in silent gray as we climb into the boat. I'm glad I've got the middle position, Thomas up front and Forrester behind. I don't like the idea of disappearing within the folds of the fog, and it's reassuring to know these two will keep me anchored between them.

I haven't been in a canoe for a while, but it doesn't take long to catch the rhythm of paddling through the smooth water. We glide into the morning, and I breathe deep, trying to keep my head clear but unable to stop the thoughts playing on an incomplete loop, like the end of a film reel flapping against my brain.

Bea is pregnant. And it has nothing to do with me, but it affects the people I love. Brandon is going to be an uncle before he even reaches his seventeenth birthday, and I have a sickening feeling that once his parents find out, they'll put extra pressure on him not to "screw up" like his sister. Which, pregnancy-wise, shouldn't be a problem. Still, if they knew I'm the one he sneaks into his bedroom when they're not around, I don't think they'd be thrilled.

And Brandon's only one half of the equation. The other is Thomas. He's not panicking, at least not externally. The baby is not likely his, a probability I'm sure he's clinging to. But the possibility, however slim, still exists. And I hope he'll be there if she winds up needing his help.

I focus on the stroke of my paddle, liking the way it pulls heavily through the water and then floats up above the surface. Heavy tug, weightless float. Tug, float. Heavy, weightless.

"So," Forrester says a long time after we've set out, "when are you leaving for your trip?"

I rub my nose, its tip like ice against the back of my hand as Thomas answers.

"Next weekend, I think," he says.

I'm annoyed by the way Forrester has asked the question, like he knows my brother's going is a certainty. And I'm frustrated at how quick Thomas was to respond, like he's not even considering altering his plans with the new information he's received.

"I could leave at any time," Thomas continues, his voice far too easy for the topic at hand. "But I need a few days to make some initial plans. Figure out which direction I'm headed, where my first major stop will be."

"Sounds great," Forrester says from his spot behind me.

I don't turn to look at him, focusing instead on a splash in the water to our left. A fish, maybe, or a beaver. I wait for a repeat jump as we move by.

"You know, I have an empty passenger seat," Thomas says after a beat.

For a second I almost snort, thinking he's offering the spot to me. But then I realize that I'm not an active participant in this discussion, that I'm only here to witness the decisions being made.

My frustration should be growing as I notice how unburdened Thomas's voice is when he extends the casual offer to our cousin. But it doesn't. Something in my brother's tone shivers down my spine, and for the first time I think there might be a good cause behind his plans for departure.

I remember the night when Thomas explained to me where he'd been for the week he'd disappeared, why he'd vanished without a word. I'd been furious and hurt at the beginning of that conversation, but by the end I'd idolized my big brother in a way I never had before.

In the canoe now, I stay silent, forcing even my thoughts to sink down until they are nothing more than soft ripples in the water.

"I can't offer much," Forrester replies. His words are soft. "A bit of money. An unimpressive bit of company, I imagine. And a canoe."

Thomas lets out a quiet laugh. "Sounds like a winning combination to me."

They don't say anything more, and I make no effort to question their motives or argue against the proposal. As far as companions go, Forrester will be a good one for Thomas. His presence is unobtrusive. Sitting behind me, he's like something solid and heavy, but something that doesn't pull us down. A tree, maybe. Quiet and still, with strong, living roots that dig deep into the earth. Thomas needs that, even if he doesn't think so. And if Forrester's asking to join Thomas's trip, it's because the trip is one he needs to take.

With any luck, Bea is pregnant with Rodge's child. He will be there for her, and I will be there for Brandon. And, if it all plays out like it should, Thomas will be free to be there for Forrester. I hate the idea of my brother taking off for an extended trip of who-knows-what and who-knows-where. But I'm not so bothered knowing my cousin will be by his side, keeping him tethered.

Forrester's brought his fishing equipment with him, and we canoe to a favorite spot of his for a few minutes of trying to catch a bite. He and Thomas cast and reel as I relax into the canoe. Geese fly above us, and there's more unidentified splashing far out near the shoreline. The quiet sounds of the early morning are enough noise for all of us.

THOMAS

I WONDER WHO THE girl is, why they're so worried about time. How she almost died. Why they even care.

I wonder where they are going to go, if they go at all. I wonder which brother will win this argument.

"If we do this, it has to be in the fall," my father says with a sigh.

I imagine him rubbing his hands over his face, his gold wedding ring glinting in the sun. I sink lower, almost to my ears, almost to the point of not hearing another word.

I don't allow myself to be swallowed by the bay. Not yet.

"That's fine," my uncle says, happiness bursting through his worry.

"Late September, October even … I can't get time off work before then."

"October will work. She likes the cooler weather."

"Okay, but you're in charge. I never could plan a trip to save my life."

"If it was up to you, you'd never go anywhere."

"I don't know why you feel the need to travel, Simon. You own a slice of paradise."

"Paradise is everywhere. In everything. If it was just me and Forrester, well … someday I'll take him on a trip, too. After this one is complete."

KAYLA

I WAKE UP TO FIND my hand resting on the soft fur of Star's back. I don't know where she came from. Last night, sometime after dinner but before pie, the dogs disappeared. Forrester said Runner likes to sleep upstairs, and I suppose Star must have been with him. They didn't even make an appearance during the midnight fiasco that brought us all to the living room.

I give the collie a few groggy pats before I turn onto my back and blink up at the bright daylight filtering down from the windows. What a night. My unexplained nightmare means nothing in the morning sun. Not after the explained craziness of Nolan's obsessive texts.

A boyfriend and a baby. Hailey must feel awful. I hope she does, anyway. I do, and it wasn't my nosing about that spilled the beans to Thomas.

I ache everywhere, but the smell of coffee and the feel of Allison's legs pressing against my feet motivates me to move. I get up as soon as I'm awake enough to coordinate my movements, my limbs begging for the relief of a full-body stretch.

"Morning," Hailey calls from the kitchen, her voice light.

She stands over the stove, something sizzling in a pan before her. I pad across the room, careful not to disturb Eli as I step over him. Thomas and Forrester must have gone on their canoe trip already. I don't see Nolan anywhere, either, so perhaps he went along, too. At least it didn't continue raining this morning. They'd be bummed about missing the opportunity to get the canoe on the water one more time before we leave.

"Morning," I yawn.

I get in a good stretch before I sit at the kitchen table, where I pull an elastic from around my wrist and gather my hair into a quick ponytail. My face is in serious need of a wash and a fresh coat of makeup, and I fear my breath is in an even more dire state. But I can't be bothered to clean up yet. I'm still tired, not to mention sore. Last night was rough.

"Something to drink?" Hailey asks.

She approaches the table with a huge pot of tea in one hand and an equally large pot of coffee in the other — the combined liquids full of enough caffeine for at least ten or twelve people. I laugh, and then I grab an empty mug and go for the teapot. I love the smell of coffee, but I only like the taste when it comes in the form of sugar-laden iced drinks. Pure coffee, steaming and rich, makes my stomach turn.

"So, what's the plan for today?" I ask while I prepare my tea. Hailey's back in the kitchen, grating cheese for what I think is an omelet. "My dad's picking me up at noon. Only a few hours left to get everything sorted."

"We only have the basement," Hailey says. "We should be able to finish before then."

"We'll do our best," I sigh. I can't stay past noon, but I don't want to leave while the others are still at work.

Allison and Eli wake up when the others return from their canoe trip. Thomas and Nolan wear matching expressions of complacency, but when they survey the rest of us it's easy to see the tired strain in their eyes. Forrester, on the other hand, walks in looking almost care-free, color in his skin and a spark in the crinkle of his eyes. He holds up a fish, and with marvelous ease he and Hailey work together to fillet and fry it for us to eat. The fish is served with toast and omelets, combinations I'm sure don't mix but which we eat in varying portions until our plates are cleared.

Last night at dinner, we talked without end. This morning, no one says much at all. Thomas and Nolan are lost in their thoughts, and the twins appear to still be tense from their own lingering argument. Hailey must feel some guilt because she's as quiet as Forrester, and I'm not prepared to break the ice by forcing inane chatter on any of us.

We've taken a step back. Last night we were a family again. Now we've resumed our positions as vague acquaintances, and it's more than uncomfortable — it reminds me too much of the way our parents behaved at Uncle Simon's funeral.

We eat, we clean dishes, and then we get dressed. I take my time in the upstairs bathroom, giving my face a thorough wash and my teeth a hard brushing. I put on my T-shirt and jeans, and then I begin brushing out my hair. We're on a deadline, but I don't rush getting ready. I idle upstairs, holding onto the cottage for every second I can.

The walls of the bathroom are a soft shade of lavender, which must have been Aunt Shirley's choice. An empty vase is on the sink — one I'm sure used to contain fresh flowers — and the mirror is surrounded by a decorative frame of white-painted wood. The space is feminine, designed for the woman not dead but still recently lost to me.

I wish my aunt were here instead of a country away, ignoring her son. I refuse to accept she's as evil as Hailey believes. After all, she left Forrester's dad the cottage when she walked out. If she'd wanted to be cruel, she could have taken this place from Simon during the divorce. Even if she'd tried and failed, the costs of fighting may have forced my uncle to cut his losses and sell the cottage, anyway. I don't think she tried to take it, though. I think she left it because she knew what it meant to them, and that says something.

But then again, if she really cared, she could spare a few hundred dollars and a couple of days away from home to fly up here and see her grieving son.

People make no sense.

When my hair is knot-free, my teeth are smooth, and my eyeliner's been smudged the right amount, I sit on the edge of the dirt-stained porcelain tub and stare at the purple walls. The bathroom is nice — a little outdated, but bright and airy thanks to the pretty color and the big window overlooking the forest out front. The same could be said for most of the rooms here. At its heart, this bathroom is a good representation of the whole cottage. A little outdated, but still remarkable.

The seven of us being here this weekend feels that way, too.

When I go downstairs, Forrester is standing by the staircase leading to the basement. The twins are on the back porch, Allison stretching and Eli pacing. Hailey's in the kitchen still, wiping down the counters, and Nolan's on the living room couch, surprisingly enough without his phone. I hear water running in the powder room, and soon see Thomas strolling down the hall, shirt off and a toothbrush in his mouth.

"Don't leave the water running," Nolan calls before Thomas even makes it into his brother's line of sight. Thomas sighs, spinning on his heel and returning to the powder room. The water shuts off as I join Forrester with a smile.

"I always thought it'd be nice to have a brother or sister," he admits.

Forrester's the only one in our family who's an only child, at least on our dads' side. I don't know about my aunts' families. Thinking about my cousins having other cousins I'm not related to is weird. My mom is one of three kids. Her brother's single with no children, but her sister has four kids of her own. They live in Manitoba, and they come here or we go there about once every other year. Her kids are all younger than me, though. The oldest is twelve now, the youngest only six. When we're visiting, being around them is more like baby-sitting than anything else.

"Having a sibling's awesome and awful," I say, as Thomas reappears fully clothed, his toothbrush ready to be stuffed back into his bag. "But I like it."

"How is Tate, anyway?" Forrester asks. He looks troubled, his eyes moving from me to Hailey in the kitchen. "I never even thought to ask. Sorry … I didn't mean to forget, I just …"

"Tate's fine," I interject, putting my hand on his arm. "So are Marissa and Liam, as far as I can tell. There's a lot of missed ground to go over. It'll take a while for us to get caught up."

"Yeah." Forrester nods. He runs a hand through his hair and lets out a deep billow of breath. Then he raises his voice so the others can hear. "We should get going on the basement."

Hailey leaves the kitchen and the twins come inside — Eli worn out, Allison refreshed. With a full stomach and sore limbs, I follow behind Hailey and Eli as we head back down into the rec room to begin the final stage of cleanup. For a minute, I survey the room as if we hadn't spent hours down here last night, studying the outstretched sofa bed, the strewn cushions, the snack foods and empty pie dish left over from our evening dessert. The evidence of our presence is like something straight from a memory. The last memory of its kind we'll have in this room. Even if the cottage weren't being sold, we'd never have another night like the evening now gone.

One of the most vicious realities of life is that we can't get back to the past. Time keeps rolling forward, and we're left to survive on memories unable to keep up. This place, messy and outdated, is a miracle of time travel.

The room is well deserving of a moment of appreciation, but my reverie is soon interrupted by Thomas.

"Okay, let's do this!" he calls.

He barrels down the stairs behind me, and I jump out of the way to avoid getting bowled over.

Thomas claps his hands together, his smile far too cheerful. He's decided to play at being happy, and watching his effort is exhausting. Still, I don't see any other way of getting things accomplished today, not if we ever want to move past the awkwardness left over from this morning's earliest hours. So, I let my eyes sweep across the painting over the fireplace for a few lingering seconds, and then I step into the room with a smile of my own.

"Does the stereo still work?" Nolan asks.

He heads straight for the sound system next to the TV.

"Should." Forrester shrugs, moving over to the box of movies. "Won't get any reception for the radio, and there's no Bluetooth. CD player's fine, but I warn you the selection is even worse than the movie choices."

"I'm sure we can find something." Nolan smirks.

He sets about rifling through the CD cases as the rest of us get to work. Forrester and Thomas collect the VHS tapes from the floor, placing them back in their cases while Hailey and I strip the sheets from the sofa bed.

"What are you going to do with all these movies?" Eli asks, watching the others dump tapes into the big box.

Forrester shrugs again, his head lowered, his dark golden-brown hair obscuring the view of his eyes.

"Throw them out. No market for VHS anymore, and there's nothing here you can't get for cheap elsewhere."

"I doubt you can find *The Peanut Butter Solution* on Netflix." Allison laughs.

"Well, maybe I'll keep that one," Forrester says, but he doesn't take the movie out of the box.

"Not my first choice, but it'll have to do," Nolan mutters.

He lifts a CD from a cracked and scratched case, eyeing the underside of the disc before popping it into the stereo.

"I suppose that's true," Eli says, his gaze still set on the box of movies. "VHS tapes like these are worthless now. Seems a waste, though."

"You're free to have them if you want," Forrester says, his voice an odd mix between bothered and unconcerned. "I'm not keeping them for my own sake. I hardly ever watch movies."

The grungy strum of a guitar sounds out from the stereo, followed by the upbeat tempo of a beating drum. I pause in my work on the bedsheets, listening as a man's voice begins singing an indie rock tune.

"My parents used to love this album." I smile.

Nolan glances over his shoulder at me.

"Ours, too," he says, nodding.

"I know this song," Allison says, snatching the CD case from Nolan. "Sloan? Never heard of them. Why is this so familiar, though?"

"We used to listen to it during the summers here," I say.

I bend back down to continue my task, folding the sheets into neat, off-white squares.

"Did we?" Allison looks at the case before placing it back on the TV stand. "I don't remember. Well, maybe I do a bit."

"It's a good CD. If peppy alt-rock fits your tastes," Thomas says as he closes the flaps of the cardboard movie box. "I'll take the movies back with me and get rid of them later," he adds to Forrester. "You've got enough to take in your car as it is."

"Thanks." Forrester nods as he turns to unplug the TV set.

We put the sheets in a pile by the stairs, and then we fold the bed into its frame before fitting the cushions back into place. When we make the first trip up to load the TV and the box of movies into the cars, Allison goes to the kitchen to collect cleaning supplies.

"You don't want to leave the TV for staging?" Eli asks as Forrester hauls the old thing outside, Thomas grabbing the back to help steady the weight. "It'll make the room a bit unbalanced, won't it?"

"Oh, don't start your design detailing now," Hailey says.

"It'll sell better with good staging!" Eli argues, not even questioning how she knows of his interest in design.

Hailey rolls her eyes.

"It won't need any help getting sold," she says.

I'm sure she's right. The cottage might have an outdated decor, but that doesn't change the fact it's well built and situated on a gorgeous property. Nothing beats a place like this, and buyers will clamor to get their hands on it.

"I've got a friend who wants to buy the TV," Forrester says. "Figured I might as well take it back with me now and get the money."

"We can take out the entire TV stand," Hailey suggests. "Then no one will even know the TV is missing."

"That could work," Eli adds, sounding something close to excited. "We can reposition the couch across from the fireplace. That's where it should be, anyway. Right by the fire — make that the centerpiece of the room. Less a recreational space, more a sophisticated lounge. People will like that."

"You sound like you've given this thought," Hailey says, her eyebrows raised in question.

Eli rakes shaggy hair to one side of his forehead and places his hands on his hips in an almost defiant pose.

"They're actually my dad's thoughts," he mumbles. "Back then, every trip home from the cottage he'd spend at least half the time talking about how much he would change if he owned the place. I think it drove him insane it belonged to Simon."

"Funny, isn't it?" Hailey says, letting her breath out in a long sigh. "When we're kids, we think our parents are just, you know, our parents. And parents know best. They're always right, and they don't have any flaws ... except when they don't let you do what you want. Nothing major, though. Nothing earth-shattering. But then you grow up."

"And suddenly you realize they're just people," Nolan cuts in.

"You see them as people, not as parents. And as people, they're not perfect."

"Nowhere near it," Allison mutters, joining the conversation as she meets us out on the back porch, rags and spray bottles in hand. "How is that fair? Shouldn't we always see our parents as perfect? Isn't that our right — their right, too?"

"How will we ever learn from our mistakes if we can't see them played out across the generations?" Hailey asks.

Eli scoffs.

"We still don't learn, even when we do see it," he says.

I'm not sure whether it's Eli's words or the cold snap outside that makes me shiver. As Thomas and Forrester push the TV into the Jeep, I hug my arms to my chest and wonder at how fast the temperature dropped overnight. Autumn is here today, and it makes me excited for the second round of turkey and trimmings I'll have with my parents and a group of their friends tonight. But the excitement is bitter-sweet. Along with it comes annoyance that this family holiday will be spent with family friends instead, and I can't escape the depressing weight of knowing Hudson won't be in attendance, either.

The bite of the breeze feels like worry, too — worry I'll slip back into my normal life at home and leave all of this behind as if it's nothing more than a momentary glitch in time.

When the TV is loaded up, we go back to the basement and dismantle the rest of the stand. The stereo is left on the floor until everything else has been packed away, and then we shut Sloan off and bring the stereo up as well. Allison takes charge of the bathroom, and Hailey pulls out the clunky old vacuum I'm stunned still roars to life. Eli pushes the furniture around with Thomas's help, and we pick up all the last odds and ends until the basement looks neat and un-lived-in.

"I think that's it," Forrester says from the bottom of the stairs as he surveys the finished room.

The set-up is strange with the sofa facing the fireplace and the TV gone — like we're standing in someone else's room, gathered in the basement of a stranger's house.

My eyes settle on the painting as my cousins start up the steps, and I move to the mantelpiece to straighten the frame before we go. I drag the far bottom corner over an inch, the weight more unsteady than I expected. The painting rocks a little, like it might wobble and fall, before settling into place. When I let my fingers go, however, the weight tips the whole frame back to its previous position, the painting drooping on the left side.

"It might need to be adjusted at the top," Forrester says, eyeing the painting like it's a stubborn pet.

He steps over to help me lift the frame so we can adjust where the wire hangs on its thick nail. But as we move the painting out from the wall, something bumps, jostles, and tumbles onto the mantelpiece before dropping to the floor.

I gasp, worried we've ruined the beautiful landscape, until I realize that what fell was a small, zippered leather folder. Forrester frowns and bends to retrieve the item, and I walk my fingers across the length of the painting to feel the slit in the backing paper where the journal must have been stuffed.

"This is my dad's," Forrester says, confused. He turns the folder over, and then fingers the gold zipper along its edge. "He used these for his calendar and receipts and stuff. I don't know why he'd have put one behind the picture."

"Why don't you open it and find out?" Hailey suggests, her intent innocent but her voice still bordering on sarcastic.

"Probably just more receipts," Forrester says with a nod as he unzips the case and looks at the contents. "Receipts, construction contracts, or just a bunch of …"

I glance away from the painting as Forrester trails off. When my eyes reach his face, I see it's drawn and white.

"Forrester?" I ask.

Hailey puts a hand on his arm.

"Hey, what is it?" she half-whispers, rubbing the sleeve of his black knit sweater.

Forrester shakes his head.

"It's …" He pauses, drawing something out of the folder. "It's Julie."

"What?" Hailey crowds next to him, looking over his side at the contents within the case. Her eyes widen when they take in the sight before her. "Oh, shit," she mumbles, her hand still grasping his arm.

"What about Julie?" Thomas asks from halfway up the stairs.

He leans over the banister, straining to see what's in the folder. I step toward Forrester, my eyes trained on the black leather shaking in my cousin's grip. I reach for it, wisp my fingers against it, before Forrester speaks again.

"She's dead," he says. I pause, my hand falling back to my side. Forrester looks up, and I'm the closest, so I'm the one he makes eye contact with. "And she's family."

HAILEY

MY EARS RING WITH the stupid saying my dad always uses when the world flips upside down. *Hell's bells and a shitload of spells.*

Hell's bells, indeed.

The death certificate is enough of a shock on its own. But the other document — the *birth* certificate — piques my interest more.

Julie Annabelle Hacher. *Hacher.* Julie was one of us. She belonged to our family.

Forrester unfolds the birth certificate, but it's not one of the small blue cards I'm used to seeing, the ones we keep stored in a fireproof safe at home — the kind my mother doesn't have, or at least won't let me see. This one is longer, a folded document on creamy paper stating not only Julie's birth information but also her parentage.

Her link to us all is far closer than I'm comfortable with.

"That's Grandpa," I say in a husky voice, pointing to the man listed as Julie's father. I never met him, but he's still Grandpa — still mine.

"But that's not Grandma," Kayla adds, leaning over the folder and reading the certificate upside down.

"What?" Thomas sounds bewildered.

"Was it a first marriage? Did our grandfather have a first marriage?" Eli asks, his voice tight.

I look at the birth date. February 22, 1976. I don't know the exact birthdates of all my relatives. But I know enough to figure out this date doesn't give any sound answer to Eli's question.

"She was born between brothers," I say. I try to keep my voice even, but it wavers on the last note. "Somewhere in the middle, I think. During the marriage, for sure."

"But she wasn't Grandma's daughter?" Kayla asks, sounding confused.

She glances up at me, but I avert my gaze and stare back at the sheet. She must make her way to staring at Allison instead because the girl heaves a sigh of annoyance.

"He had an affair," she says matter-of-factly. "He had a child out of wedlock. Our grandmother must have gotten over it, so it shouldn't surprise you."

"Yeah, except it should," Nolan replies. "This woman was our aunt. We never knew our dads had a sister."

"Half-sister," Thomas corrects.

Nolan shrugs his comment away.

"Sister enough to take her photo and have her at Christmas," he argues.

"Until she screamed," Kayla says. "Then she wasn't around anymore."

"I think I might have an answer for that," Forrester says. "Or, at least part of an answer. Look at this."

He hands me another sheet. This one is a hospital record. Well, not a hospital, but something close to it. A clinical home, with medical records and admittance papers.

"She lived in a group home," I tell the others. "Looks like she was there for a number of years, anyway. I wonder what happened to her mother."

"Maybe she died, too," Kayla suggests.

"Or maybe she didn't want to care for someone with a disability," Allison counters.

"Disability?"

I raise my head, my idiotic brain making connections it should've made the moment I saw the first picture of Julie yesterday. *Fluorescent lights and a high-pitched giggle.* I did my high school volunteering in a long-term care facility, gaining experience I thought would be useful for the nursing career that never panned out. One woman who lived there had Rett syndrome. I can't believe I didn't see it before. Julie's body, the way her head was small, the way she had to be fed by someone else. The screaming.

Hell's fucking bells. *The screaming.*

"There's a neurological disorder called Rett syndrome," I say to the others. "It mostly affects girls, I think. And —" I squeeze my eyes shut, trying to pull facts out of my stupid, stupid brain. "And those with the condition are prone to outbursts of laughing, or sometimes screaming." I open my eyes and look at my cousins. "Julie must have had it. Why didn't I notice before? She probably lived in the home, and Grandpa took her out for family visits. Our parents must have decided her outbursts were too frightening for us kids, though. Might explain why we never saw her after that day. She didn't disappear ... she just disappeared from us."

"Until she died," Eli reminds me.

I sigh, looking back at Forrester's folder.

"Until she died," I agree.

I pull out the death certificate and look at the cause of death. *Asphyxiation.* She died of choking, which fits with Rett syndrome. As the disorder progresses, sufferers lose the ability to chew and swallow. Choking's not uncommon.

"I feel awful," Kayla says. "I was terrified of her, but she ..."

"You were young," Thomas cuts in. "We all were. We didn't understand."

"And why didn't we?" I ask, my voice harsh, although it's not anyone here I'm angry with. "Why didn't we see her again after that day? Why didn't we get the chance to learn and understand?"

"Because our parents didn't want us to be scared?" Nolan suggests.

"Or maybe because she was an illegitimate child," Eli mutters.

"Shut up, Eli," Allison snaps. "It didn't seem to bother them, so it shouldn't bother you."

"I'm sure it bothered our grandmother!" Eli steps close to his twin, staring her down like he might start brawling with her at any second. "I'm sure she wasn't too happy her husband cheated and kept the evidence around for everyone to see."

"Maybe he had a good reason for cheating," Allison argues. She sounds uncomfortable, like she doesn't quite believe her own words.

"Yeah, like Dad does?" Eli asks, his speech rigid. "What brilliant reasons might those be? Was Julie's mother nice and young, only seven years older than our dad was? Or did our grandfather just think she was a good piece of ass?"

I don't know what Grandpa thought, but right now *I* think my mouth might be gaping like one of the fish out in the bay. So, this is what they've been fighting about all weekend. Uncle Joey's having an affair. With a twenty-something. And his teenage children know about it.

"Hell's bells" is no longer sufficient for how messed up this weekend has become.

"Maybe we stopped seeing Julie because she died," Forrester says, his voice a soft murmur under the twins' fight.

Allison starts to respond to Eli's rant, but I hold up a hand to quiet her as I turn back to Forrester.

"What did you say?" I ask.

Forrester only shrugs, staring at the papers before him.

"When did she die?" Kayla asks, looking at me with anticipation.

Like it would make any difference. Even if Julie died the very night of the screaming, it wouldn't make me feel any better about the terror I've subconsciously harbored all these years.

Forrester hands me the death certificate. I guess I'm the town crier for these horrible declarations. If it was anyone else handing off the responsibility, I'd tell them to shove it and walk away.

But it's Forrester, so I take the paper and pinpoint the date of Julie's death.

"September 5, 2006," I say aloud. "So no, it was a few years after the screaming." I look up at my cousins to see all of my cousins staring back at me. No one says anything. For a minute I assume they're taking the news in, but when they continue to watch me, I realize their gazes are expectant. "What?" I ask, looking back down at the sheet. "There's nothing else, that's it. September 5, 2—"

"2006," Forrester finishes. I gaze at him, and he gazes at the paper. "Ten years ago."

"So, what does that have to do with anything?" I ask.

Halfway through the question I've already found my answer. Ten years ago. The last time any of us saw one another.

"Could it be coincidence?" Nolan asks, ignoring my needless question.

"I don't think so," Forrester says.

He looks through the folder again, searching for more clues.

Allison sounds perplexed.

"So, she died, and our dads stopped talking to each other?" She shakes her head, her skinny arms folded across her chest. "Why?"

"Maybe the grief was too strong," Nolan offers.

Kayla's quick to shoot down his suggestion.

"If they were overcome with grief, we'd see the memories of Julie everywhere," she says. "Have any of you ever seen a picture of her at your house? They took the photos, we have proof of that. But has any parent mentioned her ... has anyone seen a photo or a keepsake or a home movie?"

"Not us," Thomas says.

He bites the thumbnail of his left hand, and I remember Forrester on the park bench the day of his dad's funeral, biting his nail before he told us of his parents' divorce. I bit my nails until I was twelve, my mother's scolding so incessant I stopped to avoid any more fighting on our monthly night of stargazing. Watching Thomas now and remembering Forrester a week ago tempts me to pick up the old habit — the yearning like what starving dieters must feel when they see someone sitting down to a gourmet meal.

"Us neither," Eli says, looking at Kayla. "And you're right. Grief would have made her presence more prominent. Instead she was shut away in a box of old clothes and some pictures buried in a forgotten container."

"Maybe they were glad to be rid of her," Allison says then. I shoot her a dirty look, but she doesn't flinch away from my dark expression. "I know it sounds bad, but it could be true. They could have felt obligated to take care of her after Grandpa's death. After her death, maybe they were relieved and put aside all the memories of her so they could pretend she didn't exist. Maybe that's why they stopped talking, too. Out of guilt."

I'm desperate to argue against her bitchy accusation about our parents, but it's hard to find a plausible reason to suppose she's wrong. As twisted as what she's proposing is, it would explain everything, which makes her idea better than any other scenario we've come up with over the past two days.

But Forrester puts my aching mind to rest when he cuts in with words firm and certain.

"No," he says in his deep voice. "If that was the case, my dad never would have kept her clothing in the attic. It wasn't stored by accident. Those boxes were the only ones up there. Dad wouldn't have gone through the trouble if he'd wanted them gone forever. He should have thrown them out, but he didn't. He kept them for a reason."

"What if they were put up there while she was still alive?" Allison asks.

"That wouldn't make any sense," I chime in, relieved to have an argument to cling to. "If she was still alive, she'd have been wearing the clothes. Or they still would've been thrown out. It's not like they were designer pieces. They were well worn and old. They were worthless, except to whoever put them in the attic. Except to Uncle Simon."

Eli sighs. "So, we still don't know why they stopped talking."

He sits down halfway up the stairs.

"But we do know who Julie was," Kayla says.

"And we have a good guess that her death was the reason for the fight," I add.

"We just don't know how," Forrester mumbles.

His eyes scan the remaining documents in the folder.

"Anything in there that might help us figure it out?" Thomas asks.

Forrester pulls out another sheet, this one a torn piece of yellow notebook paper.

"Just this," he says, handing the sheet to me. "I'm not sure it'll be of much use, though."

The writing on the sheet is difficult to read. Not only was it done in a shaking half-print and half-cursive hand, it was written in pencil, which has now faded almost to the point of illegibility. I have to hold it up toward the overhead light and squint to work out what the words say. With considerable effort, I see what I think is supposed to read *Simcoe Courthouse, November 7, 10:00 a.m.*

"It could be unrelated," Forrester says over my shoulder.

"Yeah, it could," I agree. "But it's the best shot we've got. Nothing else in the folder to give us a clue about what happened at the courthouse?"

"No, that's all there is," Forrester says. "The only other thing is a map."

"A map?" Thomas says, sounding surprised.

Forrester nods. He takes out the folded paper, his eyes wandering over its front.

"Looks like there's a route drawn on it, but ... I don't know for what."

He hands the map to Thomas before zipping the folder shut. Thomas takes the rumpled paper, pressing his fingers along its front with a frown. He turns the map over, opens the well-creased fold, and then his mouth twists with curiosity as he pries something off the inside page.

"There's this, too," he says. He holds up a small gold key with a brown tassel hanging from its end. It must have been taped to part of the map. "Any idea what it could be for?"

Forrester looks heavy with confusion as he shakes his head. Thomas gives him the key, and he studies it while the oldest member of our group traces the map's drawn route with his finger.

"I think we should check it out," Kayla says. "The court date, that is. We might not find anything, but at least then we'd know we tried."

"We don't have to," Forrester says, his tone almost apologetic. "We've … well, we've finished cleaning up. You're all free to leave now, if you want."

"We're not prisoners," I say, sliding my eyes to briefly glower at Eli. "We can stay a while longer. Can't we?"

Eli's expression isn't as pissed off as I expected it would be. He looks more jaded now, as if the revelations of the last ten minutes have knocked all the fight out of him.

He brings a fist to his mouth and lowers his gaze.

"Yeah, we can stay," he says, the words muffled against his knuckles.

If Eli's still willing to stay, there's no use even asking anyone else. For at least a little while longer, none of us are going anywhere.

ELI

Turns out infidelity runs in the family.
Fuck.

I don't care about this Julie woman. Perhaps that makes me
an asshole.
But I think I was already there,
so maybe this pushes me
into total bastard territory.

I might care later.
Who knows?
Right now I'm enraged beyond the point
of experiencing any additional emotions.

They all know our dirty secret. And Ali's not even bothered.
Of course she's not.
She wouldn't even be bothered if they knew
Dad's pulled us in,
uses us as his alibi.

He's only picking Ali up today
so he can stop at *her* house
while Ali sits in a coffee shop,
ignores the fact that Mom's at home,

oblivious,
cooking dinner and thinking her life still makes sense.

Our grandfather did it, too.
How sick is that?

I want to know if Dad was aware,
before the baby arrived
and blew everything open.

Did he care?
Was he proud of his father for getting another girl into bed?
Was he as sickened by it
as I am?

He's the bastard,
not me.
I'm just the coward
who can't build up the nerve
to tell Mom.

If Ali would join me, I'd do it.
But Ali thinks things are better with her not knowing.
Ali doesn't want her world rocked
any more than it's already been.

But shit.
Our grandfather
did it, too.

What if Dad knocks his new woman up? Would he keep
  the baby,

flaunt it around us like it's a miracle
and not a curse?

Why does history repeat itself?

I won't be like that.
I won't.
I won't.

I won't, but Ali
might.
That scares me even more than the idea of telling Mom.

Do I let family secrets eat away at us
until we don't talk anymore,
until we hide relatives and leave it to future generations
to try and work out puzzles
that should already be complete?

I'll get home before Dad and Ali do this afternoon.
It'll just be me and Mom. If I tell her ...
If I don't tell her ...
Breathe. Just breathe.
I don't want to be
a coward
anymore.

THOMAS

BOBBING IN THE WATER, my eyes closed, my spatial awareness obscured until the world is twisted — wild and moving, calm and still.

"I'll map it all out," my uncle says. "And in October we'll take her away from that damned place and go."

"Found the guns!" Forrester yells, splashing into the bay and washing me out of my hiding place.

NOLAN

B: Good morning! You awake yet?

Sitting in a circle, documents and pictures spread everywhere over the wooden boards of the living room floor, I don't have to think of the inevitable conversation Thomas and I will have on the car ride home. Turns out, solving a decade-old family mystery is a good distraction from trying to decide whether I'll scold my brother for keeping up his plans to leave or assure him Bea will be okay once he's gone.

Me: Are you kidding me? I've been up for hours, sleepyhead. We've already finished cleaning the cottage.

Preoccupied as we all are with the topic at hand, I seem to be the only one who's remembered he has a phone out here — which means I'm the hero of the hour. Hailey's got the birth and death certificates, and Kayla holds the records from the group home. Thomas studies the map, Allison and Eli search through pictures, and Forrester twirls the little key in his fingers, the brown tassels fluttering like helicopter seeds falling from the maple trees outside. But no one has me beat. In a situation like this, the World Wide Web can't be topped.

B: Wonderful. Does that mean you're on
   your way home?

"Simcoe Courthouse," I say, typing quickly so I can respond to Brandon between page loads. Connection or not, the speed is atrocious out here, so I have plenty of time to minimize my browser without anyone noticing.

Me: Not quite. Turns out we sort
    of uncovered a major
    family secret.

    We're going to do some
    detectiving before we leave.

    I can't wait to tell you later.
    It's insane!

"Do you think we'll find anything?" Kayla asks, brushing hair behind her ear as she sits cross-legged next to Hailey. "I can't fathom how we'll find what we're looking for."

"We're starting with the courthouse," Allison says. "That's a pretty good place to begin."

Kayla shoots her an annoyed glance — one Allison fails to notice — while I flip back to my results page to find it still loading.

"I know we're searching for the courthouse," Kayla says. "But how likely is it we'll find actual information about the case? We don't even know what it was about or if it has anything to do with Julie."

"Let's just get to the courthouse first," Thomas breaks in, trying to keep things mellow.

He's been weird since he discovered that map. His fingers run the length of the pen-marked route as if it's some kind of fragile treasure.

"Nothing but some general info," I mutter, scrolling through unhelpful results consisting mostly of city websites listing one-paragraph histories and an office phone number.

"Try looking for archives," Allison suggests. "I worked a job a couple of summers ago where we digitized a bunch of text records for some city archives. It's possible they've done the same thing up here."

I type in "Simcoe archives" and then flip back to my messages.

> B: This whole weekend is insane. You
> might have to make a movie about it.

> Me: You might be right. We'll
> talk storyboards later.

My knee bounces with frustration as I wait for the message to be delivered. Even a damned text takes a full minute to send out here. How do people live with connection speeds this slow?

"The archives don't have anything that recent," I sigh when I get back to the search. "I'm mostly seeing stuff from the 1800s."

"Shit," Hailey mutters. She makes a trip to the kitchen, rummaging through the fridge before bringing back two armfuls of pop and water. "So, what are we going to look for next? If the court date doesn't tell us anything …"

"We're not finished with the court date yet," Allison interjects.

Thomas grabs a can from the pile Hailey's placed in the middle of our circle. He pops the tab, the cola fizzing as the seal peels open.

"We can try newspapers. They might have something," he suggests.

> B: Sounds very romantic.

> Me: You know you love it.

"And what the hell are the papers called?" I ask.

The question is snarkier than I intended. Flicking back and forth between slow texts and even slower page loads is getting on my nerves.

"How should we know?" Allison snaps. She crosses her arms over her chest and looks vaguely similar to the girly child she once was. "None of us lives up here."

"We don't even know if the court thing happened in this area, anyway," Hailey says. "Simcoe's a region, not a specific town."

"Even if we guess right, there's no guarantee we'll find a news clipping. If the case was small, the papers wouldn't care," Eli adds.

"Well, we have to try something," Allison huffs. "Why don't we figure out which towns are a part of the region. Or find out what area the courthouse is actually in. Then we could look up that paper first."

"We don't have all day to do this, you know," Eli argues. "We can hunt through county papers at home. There's no point wasting a bunch of time pinpointing small towns on a map to try and guess which one might have been interested in an old court case."

"Why don't we do a more general search?" Kayla offers.

She sits hunched into herself, and her arms are dotted with goosebumps. We haven't put the heat on, and it's cold now compared to yesterday. If the sun were still bright, the rays might heat the room through the windows. But the clouds are rolling fast, leaving only pockets of blue sky. Kayla probably didn't pack a sweater.

"We have pretty much nothing to go by. How much more general can we get?" I say, glancing down with the buzz of my phone.

B: Strangely enough, I do.

Good luck with your detectiving.

Talk soon. xx

I smile, while across the circle, Kayla rolls her eyes.

"Instead of looking for the place, why don't we start with the person?" she says. "Open a search engine and look up Julie. Julie Annabelle Hacher. See what comes up."

Kayla's suggestion is pathetically simple, and in that regard it's perfect. I turn my smile to her as she takes a bottle of water and sits back with it, placing the bottle by her side but not unscrewing the cap.

"Julie Annabelle Hacher," I mumble, staring at the phone again as I search the name. This time the page load is quicker, and I'm scrolling through results in a matter of seconds. "Here's her obituary."

I open the link as Thomas slides close to me and peers at the phone over my shoulder. Usually this is a serious offence, one that would earn him an elbow to the stomach and a few swear words to get him out of my space. Considering the circumstances, however, I give him a pass on the elbow jab and let him look.

The obituary is short and ordinary. Printed in the *Barrie Examiner* in September 2006, it relates how she was loved and how she'll be missed. The text mentions she was predeceased by her father, our granddad, but it makes no reference to our grandma or to Julie's biological mother. No sibling names are printed, either — it only states that she was survived by five half-brothers. Four half-brothers now.

I'm surprised to see the obit has the audacity to mention her ten nieces and nephews as well — the seven of us plus Liam, Marissa, and Tate. Out of the ten of us, Tate's the only one who might stand a chance of remembering her, while Liam probably wasn't even born the last time his sisters were in her presence. The obituary makes no mention of a court case, but it does tell mourners to make donations to the Ontario Rett Syndrome Association, which confirms Hailey's diagnosis of her condition.

I read the obit aloud, and then we continue. I find a short article on some charity camp day in 2002 with Julie included in the group picture below the article's headline before I pass through a lot of unrelated pages — blogs of people named Julie or Annabelle, and a number of French websites, too. The search seems hopeless when I reach the end of the first page of results, but after continuing half-heartedly to page two, the next entry proves to be what we've been searching for.

"Family Fights for Half-Sister's Burial Rights," I recite.

I didn't think we were making much noise as we sat and waited to find something. But after I've read the article's headline, we're all so quiet I can hear the trees rustling in the wind outside and Runner's gentle panting where he and Star lounge by the back windows.

"The fight," Kayla whispers.

Hailey nods as if in agreement.

"Read the whole thing, Nolan," Thomas says.

He finishes his drink and sets the empty can on the floor behind him so he can pay attention to my words.

"After the death of their half-sister, five brothers are in court today fighting over where their sister's final resting place will be," I read. "The argument, which has divided the brothers, is over whether the deceased should be buried in the family plot in a local cemetery or in the cemetery of the deceased's hometown. The deceased, a young woman who died as a result of a lifelong disability, was born of an extramarital affair, leading the plaintiffs of the case to argue that her body has no rightful claim to the family plot."

"We have a family plot?" Hailey asks.

I think, if the situation were different, she'd be laughing right now. As it is, she looks disturbed by this new nugget of information.

"Is there anything else, Nolan?" Allison asks, ignoring Hailey's remark.

I shrug. "Just a little. It says: 'Court proceedings will begin today at the Simcoe County Courthouse.' That's it. I think the only reason it showed in the search at all is because whoever uploaded the picture they use of the courthouse labeled it Hacher v. Hacher."

"I hate that title, it's morbid," Kayla says.

"That's what the court case would have been called," Eli scoffs.

"So, now we know what they were fighting over," Hailey says. "Whether or not Julie got to be buried with the rest of the family."

"Well … did she?" Allison asks.

She looks around, but no one has a satisfactory answer.

"I didn't even know we had a family plot," Hailey sighs.

"Neither did I," Kayla agrees. "Did anyone, um …" She trails off and looks at Forrester.

He understands her unasked question and finishes it for her, though his eyes remain fixed on the gold key.

"Did anyone see my dad get buried?" he asks in a flat voice. "I didn't," he adds, though I can't tell if the addition is made out of guilt or just out of fact.

"No, we didn't," Allison says.

Thomas shakes his head, and his response is good enough to account for both of us.

"So, we still don't know," Hailey says as she stretches her legs out before her. "We're fucking useless, aren't we?"

"I'd say we've done pretty well, so far," I offer, my tone a congratulation I don't quite mean to suggest. We have done pretty damn well, but the subject doesn't lend itself to celebration.

"Well, aside from actually going to the cemetery …" Eli starts.

Before he can continue, Allison puts a hand on his arm.

"There's one more thing we can try," she says, eyeing her twin. "Dad used to be all into genealogy when we were kids, remember? We thought it was creepy, all the old photos and grave records he had."

Eli squirms with annoyance to hear his dad mentioned, but as Allison keeps talking, his expression shifts.

"You're right," he says, sounding almost relieved to have something to offer to our investigation. "There are sites to collect grave records.

I'm sure he's put the family stuff up there. If we find the cemetery, we should find information on the graves."

"I know the cemetery," Forrester says. "I haven't been there yet, but I know where Dad's buried."

"Then, Nolan, get to it," Eli exclaims.

Forrester gives me the name of the Barrie Union Cemetery, and right away I locate a website with grave records.

"If we find Julie's grave, we know she's buried with the others," Allison says.

"But if we don't?" Kayla asks. "It could mean he hasn't updated the information since then. You said this was a hobby when you were kids. I remember he used to talk about family history and stuff. Does he still do it?"

"I don't think so," Allison says. "So, maybe you'll be right. But at least there's a chance."

"Here they are."

I smile when I pull the page up. Thomas moves in close again, and I shift the screen so he can see it. There is Grandpa and Grandma's information, as well as one more grave's details.

"Is she there?" Allison asks.

Thomas and I exchange glances before we shake our heads.

Allison deflates, and Eli's eyes grow dark.

"That could still mean the records haven't been updated," Hailey offers, but when she catches my eyes her voice trails away.

"The records *have* been updated," Thomas breathes.

"How do you know? No one's died since Julie," Allison says.

"*Allison*," Kayla whispers in a sharp voice.

Allison glances at Kayla and then turns back to Thomas and me. "You mean ..."

"My dad's there, isn't he?" Forrester says. He squeezes the key tightly in his fist.

"Yeah, he's here." I nod.

"But Julie's not," Allison continues. "Which means she's not buried with everyone else."

At this point, it's easy to confirm our suspicion. I go to the grave selection site and search Julie's name without a specific cemetery attached to it. Her information comes up as soon as the page loads, in a cemetery in Bracebridge — an eternal hour away from her father and her half-brother.

"They treated her like family because our grandfather wanted them to," Allison says, her words bitter as I put down my phone and draw my knees into my chest. "But when she died, they decided she wasn't true family, after all. What a beautiful memory."

"They didn't all think that," Kayla says. She reaches over to the pile of photos in front of the twins and picks out the one of her pregnant mother feeding Julie. "That's why they were in court in the first place. Some of them — at least one of them — wanted her to be buried with the family."

"The question is, who was on which side?" I ask.

This is the part of the mystery I doubt we'll be able to solve, not without talking to our parents. I try to guess at what role Mom and Dad played in the fight. I can't imagine them denying Julie the right to be buried with her father. But despite the laid-back nature of my parents, they hold some serious views of the world I could never come to grips with. Things not said outright, yet noticed in the odd turn of phrase or little shake of the head over some story in the news. I can't put a name to it, but Thomas has commented on it in the past, and I feel it, too — there's a reason I keep Brandon's name a mere letter of the alphabet on my phone.

Maybe our parents would be against a child born out of wedlock. I don't know them as well as I sometimes think I do. Speculations are pointless. The truth of the matter is I have no idea how they would — how they did — react to a situation like this.

"My dad didn't want her in the family plot," Hailey says, her words emotionless. She shares a knowing glance with Kayla and starts working her long hair into an uneven braid. "I remember a fight my parents had once. It makes a lot more sense now. He didn't think of her as family. He wouldn't have wanted her buried with his parents."

"That's horrible," Allison says.

"The whole thing is horrible," Kayla interjects. The picture she took is still clutched in her fingers. "But you can't start hating everyone you disagree with. How do you think it would have been for them to be raised alongside a girl who was born because their dad cheated on their mom? The decision must have been impossible for each of them, and whatever they decided, they had their reasons for it. More reasons than we have any idea of."

Allison picks at one of the pimples on her face, her lips drawn tight. She's not pretty, but she could be. The swollen bumps all over her face and neck don't bother me. Her attitude is what's making her plain, the hard expressions and sour sentiments even veering her toward ugly. I hope it's this weekend and the strain of her and Eli's burden making her so miserable. I hope she gets the chance to be pretty more often at home.

"I would never abandon her like that," she says. Her words are full of spite.

"I would," Eli counters back, his voice almost the same in every regard.

He left the phrase unaltered on purpose, left the word *abandon* untouched as a challenge to his sister. She wants to argue back, but she stops herself because she knows he's telling the truth. They're so different, these two. So alike, but damn, so different.

"I think my dad was on Julie's side," Forrester says, drawing attention away from the volcano bubbling beside him. "I think that's why he had the documents. And the clothes. If I were to hazard a guess, I'd say my mother didn't like the idea of Julie being buried with Grandpa, but Dad did. I bet that's why the clothes were hidden, and …"

Forrester trails off, his brows furrowing as he opens his hand and stares at the key lying on his palm. His head tilts to one side in thought, and then, without speaking, he stands. We watch him cross the living room to where a pile of stuff waiting to be loaded into his car is stacked by the back wall of windows. Forrester rummages through a few items, and then returns to the circle, the small wooden chest from Julie's boxes in the attic clutched in both hands.

Forrester balances the box on his lap and slides the tasseled key into the lock. The key twists with ease, a soft click allowing Forrester to lift open the lid. His eyes scan over the contents of the box, and his face takes on a peculiar, blanched pallor as his lips purse tight.

"What is it?" Kayla asks, her voice hitched and breathless.

"She …" Forrester swallows hard as his eyes lift to stare between us. "She's not buried there."

"What?" Allison asks, crowding in beside him to see. "What do you mean she's not — oh *shit*."

Thomas and I share a glance before we — along with everyone else in the room — scramble over to Forrester. We cram together, and I press into my brother's shoulder to get a view of the box's interior.

On the inside of the box lid, a small plaque has been engraved with a few lines of text.

> *May the body that kept you grounded,*
> *Hold a soul that lets you fly.*
> *And as the light of your life brightened the darkest of places,*
> *So too will the strength of your memory uphold the things*
> *   that fall.*
> *Julie Annabelle Hacher*
> *1976–2006*

Nestled in the bottom of the box is a single item — a small plastic baggie that protects the coarse, gray grains of Julie's cremated ashes.

"He didn't bury her," Hailey says, something almost like a smile twitching at her lips. "Sneaky bastard."

"Hailey, this is serious," Eli scolds, but Forrester shakes his head, his own expression brightening.

"No, she's right," he says. "Dad must have taken charge of having her buried. He must have ordered a headstone, but then … he couldn't go through with it."

"So he hid her ashes at the back of the attic?" Allison barks. "Hardly seems like a better solution."

"He didn't want anyone to know what he did," Forrester says, ignoring her snarky tone. "Probably least of all my mom. So, he kept her safe until he could give her a proper resting place, or — I don't know — until he could find somewhere to scatter the remains."

Thomas puts a hand on Forrester's shoulder, his fingers squeezing hard into the fabric of our cousin's shirt.

"*The map*," he mutters.

I scoot back to give my brother space as he pushes himself up. Long legs tripping over themselves, Thomas hurries to retrieve the old map from the folder. When he returns to his spot, he unfolds the paper and puts a finger to the marked route.

"Yesterday in the bay," he says, his eyes on Forrester, "when you talked about traveling with your dad. Simon said the time had come to *let go*. That's why he wanted to take the trip. Years ago — the last summer we were here, a couple of months before Julie died — I overheard our dads talking about taking a trip, too. I never understood that conversation. Not until today. But I think they were planning to take Julie with them, while she was still alive. Maybe …" He looks at the box still poised on Forrester's lap. "Maybe your dad was still planning to take her, even after she died."

Forrester studies the ashes, one hand gripping the box as the other sweeps across the epitaph his father must have written. When he glances up at Thomas, the color is back in his cheeks and there's a liveliness in his stare that I haven't seen in … well, a decade. I'm glad. I have no reason to think Thomas's assumption is wrong. But even if I did there's no way I'd dare say anything against it. Forrester may never get another chance to learn something new about his dad. As weird as the situation has become, I'm happy this last discovery is, for him, a good one.

KAYLA

THE STORY IS NOW complete. At least, as complete as we can expect. Our fathers fought over the death of a half-sister, over whether or not to lay her to rest as a member of the family. I can't fathom how hard the decision must have been. Even in my most vivid imaginings, I doubt I could come close to feeling our parents' pain.

I wonder if Dad knew Julie's parentage when he was my age. Did he call her his sister? Did Grandpa call her his daughter? Or did they only refer to her as Julie, someone separate from the family altogether?

Would Dad be happy to know Simon kept Julie's ashes? Or would he be sickened that the court's decision was not carried out?

I love history. I want to study it in school and teach it as my career. But once again, this weekend has reminded me how little I know of my own family. Would Grandpa have been the kind of person to take a girl like Julie under his care? I never met him, so I can't say. He could have been a sweet man with a good heart who made a terrible mistake — or maybe one who fell in love with the wrong woman at the wrong time. But then again, he could have been a jerk, a serial adulterer who only happened to get caught once. For all we know, it could have been Grandma who insisted Julie stay around. The affair could have destroyed their marriage, or the lesson could have brought them back together.

I know nothing. Absolutely nothing. I made the decision to come here this weekend in part to remedy that. I'm not sure the venture has been a success, at least not yet. When I get home, whether my dad likes it or not, I'm going to ask him about the history of the Hacher family.

Of course, if I want him to talk, I suppose I should share what I've discovered, too. But I'm not sure how much I'm ready to divulge about my own family secrets.

"Should we tell them?" I ask, this thought curling around me like a scarf of shivering cold.

"Tell who?" Eli asks, before he understands. "Our fathers? What good could it do?"

"Might do some good for the ones who wanted Julie buried with the family." Hailey shrugs.

"Yeah, except we don't know what side anyone was on," Thomas reminds her.

"Forrester should decide," Nolan suggests. "It was Simon's secret. And no one else cared enough to help him make Julie's final arrangements. So, they shouldn't get a say in what happens to her now."

I'm not sure everyone agrees with the reasoning, but no one argues against it.

"Well," Forrester muses, "I think what Thomas said earlier makes sense. My dad planned to take Julie on a trip. He can't now, but I can. I will. I don't want there to be another fight between your parents. So ... I'll scatter the ashes along the way. Dad picked a route he thought she would like. I'll take her to the same places, and once that's done, she'll be gone. It won't matter if we tell them, then. At that point, they won't be able to do anything about it."

He looks to Thomas, who nods. Then he closes the box and locks it before placing it on the floor before us. For a long moment, we stare at the small rectangle of shining wood, no one making a sound.

"We should finish up and have some lunch before we go," Hailey says after the silence has fully rippled between us.

Her words are out of place, jarring after the truths we've uncovered. But the suggestion is mundane enough it stirs us into action. Without talking, we place the pictures back into the bin and then move to the kitchen to pack up the remaining food before we start collecting our personal belongings.

After I've handed back everyone's phones, I fish out my own cell and check my notifications. My stomach drops when I see no calls or texts have come from Hudson. But instead of the crushing weight I expect to set in, the lack of communication sparks a determination in me. I've already decided Dad and I are going to talk about the things he's left unsaid for so many years. So, what's stopping me from making Hudson participate in the same kind of conversation?

This weekend has brought with it a lot of uncertainties. But one thing I am sure of is the fact that unwanted silence does nothing but destroy. I love Hudson, and I'm scared about this new life the two of us are leading, about the changes he's made without me by his side. But pretending nothing is wrong won't fix the issues. Acting like I'm not afraid doesn't make the worries go away.

I put my phone back in my purse, content to let it stay quiet until I make the call when I get home. When I glance back up, I watch my other cousins as they scroll through missed notifications and stuff the phones in their pockets when they are finished catching up. All except for Forrester, who presses his phone to his ear and listens to a voicemail that's come through at some point in the last day.

"It's the agent," he relates, even while the message is still being played. "There's already been an offer on the cottage."

"Glad we did all that work sprucing the place up, then," Eli groans.

"How is there an offer already?" Allison asks with a sidelong glare at her brother. "It's not even listed yet, is it?"

Forrester shrugs. "No, not yet. But word gets around." He ends the call to his voicemail and pockets the phone. "It's a good offer. And nice that it's quick. I'll call the agent when I'm home and accept it."

"Just like that?" I ask, unable to keep the disappointment out of my voice. I knew the cottage would be sold eventually. But while we're all still standing within it? I thought we'd have a little more time — a little more distance before we had to say goodbye.

"Yep, guess so," Forrester sighs.

We return to the business of cleaning, and in the space of a few minutes we've pushed everything out onto the back porch. Forrester does a final sweep of each floor before he joins us outside, the box containing Julie's ashes held under one arm.

"Well, that's it, then," he says, shutting the door behind him without another glance inside.

"You'll be back here, though," Allison remarks, leaning against the porch door.

"No, I won't," Forrester replies. He looks at us, his shoulders shrugging even before he speaks. "I'm leaving for a while. After I take Julie on her trip … I'm not coming home."

When we continue to wait for further explanation, Thomas takes up the narrative.

"He's coming with me," the oldest of our group declares. "We're going to leave later this week. Pack up, bring the canoe with us, travel while we figure things out."

"You're not going anywhere for school? College or university or anything?" Eli asks, his eyes still trained on Forrester.

"Not that it matters," Forrester replies, "but I'm not even finished high school yet. Missing a couple of courses still. I'm eighteen, though … I don't have to go back. Doesn't bother me if I don't finish. I can do that later, if I need to."

"You need to," Hailey scolds. "You have to finish high school."

Forrester doesn't seem convinced.

"What I need is to get away from here," he says.

Hailey turns to Thomas with accusation in her eyes, and Thomas responds with a hard stare of his own.

"School isn't important for everyone, Hailey," he says, his hands pushed into the pockets of his jeans. "Some things matter more. Why should he stick around while a bank takes away his cottage? He doesn't own anything, and he'll be homeless by the end of the month. I don't know if you remember, but his change in situation didn't come with a warning. It's not something he's been preparing for."

"Shut up, Thomas," Hailey snaps.

Forrester intervenes before the two get overheated.

"It's okay, Hailey," he says, his voice calm. "Thomas is right. I didn't expect my dad to die. I didn't want him to. I still don't, and if he was alive, I would be glad to stay put and go back to school. But he's not, and I can't see spending day after day in a place I hate, trying to work part-time after classes to scrape by."

"But what about the money from the cottage?" Allison asks. "There will be enough from the sale to keep you going for a while."

Forrester shakes his head, the motion a surprise to us all.

"I don't get the money from the sale," he admits. "At least not yet. Turns out, Dad had a plan ... he was going to give me the cottage for my thirtieth birthday. The deed was in a trust fund. Now that he's gone, whatever money is left over after the mortgage is paid will go in there instead. So, I'll have a nice gift twelve years from now. In the meantime, I'm on my own. And that's why I want to leave. If I go with Thomas, I can put distance between my dad and me. I might even go and visit my mom."

"So, you're really leaving?" The question comes from Hailey, and after a second I realize it's directed not at Forrester, but at Thomas. "Even with ..."

Thomas nods, leaving her words to sink away.

"I'm going crazy here," Thomas says.

He's not speaking to his brother, but nevertheless Nolan nods as well, their gestures identical. This must have been the ending Nolan suspected, even if it's not the one he wants.

Allison pushes herself away from the door and steps further out onto the porch. In the light of a momentary ray of sun, her blond hair appears almost white.

"We shouldn't spend any more time moping," she says, her voice almost vacant. "We should enjoy the property until we've got to leave."

"That sounds good," Forrester agrees.

When he smiles, I think the expression's genuine.

I'm cold when we head down to the fire pit again. I can't believe only yesterday my cousins were swimming in the bay. Today I doubt even Thomas would make such a dive. The breeze is so chilled it smells sharp like snow, and I wouldn't be surprised if tomorrow I woke up to find frost on the grass in our backyard.

I suck up my discomfort, huddling into myself until the fire's started and I can inch close to the flames.

"What are we having for lunch, then?" Forrester asks, stoking the fire with expert ease.

"S'mores," Hailey says, grinning, already digging for supplies.

"It's way too early for s'mores," Allison protests.

Hailey shakes her head, her black braid flying.

"It's never too early for s'mores," she replies. "And I didn't get any last night. You don't come to the cottage and not have s'mores."

"Agreed."

I smile, taking a bar of chocolate and ripping into the purple foil packaging.

"The last s'mores," Forrester says with a small chuckle. "And the last fire."

"Let's make it a good one, eh?" Thomas nods.

Not even Allison has anything to say against that. Hailey passes around the crackers and the marshmallows, and we each pick and choose our personal favorite chocolate to use. We compile our creations and argue over whether open-faced or two-cracker s'mores are the best. Eli doesn't leave his first marshmallow in the fire long enough, and Forrester leaves his in until it catches bright with flame. Hailey gets chocolate all over her lips and doesn't care. Nolan gets marshmallow stuck between his fingers and wipes the goo on his brother's jeans.

For the next hour, the final hour, we sit in the chairs we started this weekend in, eating and laughing and saying goodbye to the memories we'll never again create here.

HAILEY

WHILE WOLFING DOWN MY fourth not-regretting-a-moment s'more, I think about Forrester leaving with Thomas. I don't like the idea of either of them being so far away from the rest of us. We just got them back, damn it. I can't stand the thought of letting all this unravel again so soon.

But I appreciate what Thomas is willing to do for his cousin. There are stories, folklore I've flipped through in the books I've started to collect, full of betrayal and comeuppance. People being cruel, and people being devoured by the wild for their cruelty. But there are stories, too, of families being strong, and of foundlings lost in the woods rescued by well-meaning wolves.

Thomas isn't a wolf. But Forrester is lost, and I'm glad he's found someone to keep him company.

"What are you going to do with everything left in the cottage?" Allison asks, looking at Forrester while she pulls gooey marshmallow from her twig and plops it in her mouth. "I mean, after the sale's gone through," she adds in a full-mouthed mumble.

Forrester hunches his shoulders up and forward, the motion both defensive and careless.

"Sell it all. Let the bank decide what to do with it."

"What about the painting?" Kayla asks.

She sits close to the fire, trying to keep warm. The temperature has nosedived, the cold air nothing like the warmth of the rest of this month. The storm swept summer away, all right. I love it, but I'd be less enthusiastic if I didn't have my shawl.

Forrester's surprised by her question.

"*October Gold*?" he asks.

By the name I assume they're talking about the painting in the basement. Kayla looked at it a lot last night and this morning. She must like it.

Pictures of landscapes are okay, I guess, though I much prefer paintings of the night sky swirled with wind and speckled with stars. Still, the basement's landscape caught my attention, too, even before we discovered Julie hiding in its backing. Reminded me of a picture in my parents' room, except theirs is of a town, not the woods. I'm not sure why the two connected in my brain. Something familiar about the style, perhaps.

"Is that what it's called?" Kayla asks with a smile.

"Yeah." Forrester nods, before shaking hair from his dark eyes. "I only know because I saw the original on a field trip once. Most boring field trip I've ever been on, but cool to see the painting. I thought the name sucked, though. Spent the rest of the day trying to come up with a better one."

"And?"

I quirk a brow and wait for his response, but he only laughs, the noise more breath than sound.

"I didn't come up with anything. That's the day I realized I'm not a creative person."

"So, you're just leaving everything behind?" Allison asks.

She sticks another marshmallow on her twig and pokes it toward the fire. For arguing against the early sugar-invasion, Allison's had twice as many marshmallows as anyone else.

"Pretty much." Forrester shrugs. "The bank will sell it, put what-ever's made into my account. There won't be a lot, but at least I'll have access to it now. It'll be enough to help get me started. Whenever I decide what I want to start."

He's quiet for a minute, watching as Runner and Star play near the docks. Star's going to need a serious grooming session once we're home. I'm dreading the ride back. My car's going to reek of mud and wet dog for days.

"Do you want the painting, Kayla?" Forrester continues once Runner's circled Star twice, bolted away, and has flopped down on his stomach waiting for her to catch up with his long strides.

"Seriously?" Kayla asks, her face bright. "I'd love it. If you don't mind not getting the money for it."

Forrester smiles.

"The bank won't get anything close to its worth, anyway," he says. "It's yours. I'll make sure it's sent to you once the place has sold." He looks up at the cottage now locked away from us. "I guess it won't be long."

I follow his gaze and let my eyes sweep up to the attic, where Julie was tucked away for years, forgotten by everyone but Simon. Stories of rescued foundlings are nice, but the reality for those lost or defenseless is usually far grimmer.

Forrester has found someone to take him in, but Julie never did. She couldn't have had it easy, being surrounded by her half-brothers, so close to a family she couldn't really call her own. I have no reason to believe Julie was anything other than gentle. I doubt she was capable of deception or cruelty. But in the end, she was left on her own, kept at a distance until she was dead and supposedly buried far from those who shared her blood.

The s'mores congeal at the base of my throat as I stare at the attic window. I don't believe in ghosts, but I have this weird thing about places being haunted. A spirit isn't needed to make somewhere foreboding. All I have to do is look at the way my mother cringes when she hears talk of a reservation to know that.

My soul aches for Julie, for the others like her, and for those treated far worse. I remember the hours I spent volunteering at the care facility, how disgusted I could sometimes be by the families who only pretended to care and the ones who didn't even bother to do that. The world is full of love, but it's also full of hate, and most disturbing of all is the abundance of indifference. My mother went through pain, but at least the pain taught her how to work hard to create a new life where pain is kept to a minimum. She holds hate in her bones, but at least when she smiles over her morning coffee as she watches my siblings getting ready for school, I know her happiness is real.

Fuck. Never before has it occurred to me that, in some sick and twisted way, my mother is one of the lucky ones. She had the option of running away from the horror. She was capable of getting up, opening her front door, and leaving it all behind.

People like Julie don't have that option. Not everyone has the same ability. Some are too selfish — or selfless — to risk the unknown and go. Some aren't brave enough or strong enough to even make the decision to leave. And some simply don't have the physical, emotional, or mental capability to escape.

I breathe in the cold air and try not to throw up, my no-regret lunch now taunting me with a heavy sweetness sinking hard into my stomach. I can't look at the cottage anymore. Inside those walls exists a family, one alive and whole and happy. Out here, a brother and a sister are dead. Nothing is whole, and I'm so full of the wrongness of life I want to scream and kick and give every single asshole I can find a personal "fuck you."

The time has come for me to go home. I'm tired, and there's a shitload of work I still need to do — starting with talking to my mother. I've never been grateful for the pain she endured to give me a happy life. But at the same time, she doesn't understand the pain she's inflicted by denying me the chance to know my own heritage. The Hacher family was nearly destroyed by secrets and silence. I can't let that happen to the other half of my lineage, too. Fear be damned.

I need to learn at least a little about the life my mother used to lead. And I need her to hear — without yelling or cursing or slamming of doors — why my identity will never be as one-sided as hers.

So, we'll talk. And when that is over, I will write my professor and make arrangements for the trip I've been too scared to take. Then I will mourn my aunt and use her memory to bolster my drive as I start making a better mark upon this shitty world.

ELI

Hailey's the first to suggest
leaving.
I assumed she'd stay till the end, but in a few short minutes
her attitude changes from easy
to impatient.

Something freaked her out, but I'm not sure what.
Not that I mind.
Dad's not here yet, but I'm not waiting for Ali to leave before
   I head off.
I want to get home
with plenty of time to talk to Mom.

Ali would kill me if she knew what I was planning.
But I have new truths to live with,
new memories to sort in my mind.

I still don't know why Dad yelled,
why Mom cried,
why they were both so miserable in the half-remembered
   vision
Julie brought to light.

But I understand she was the reason,
and I can't let the same thing happen to my future,
can't cause the family I may someday have
the same kind of suffering.

Which is why Mom and I
need to have a conversation

before Ali gets home
and gets in my way.

I should have been the first to leave.
Everyone would have expected as much.

I don't know why I hesitated
until Hailey moved toward the cars,
calling her dog
and hauling her stuff into the back seat.

I've been looking forward to getting home all weekend.
So why am I lingering still,
taking my time getting my things put away,
hanging around while Hailey hugs us all?

I should go.
I should get in the car
and go.
But I don't.
I wait my turn
to hug Hailey,
too.

Fuck, what am I turning into?
Looks like I'm going to
miss these people,
after all.

KAYLA

"DO YOU WANT TO get together next weekend?" Hailey asks as she hugs me tight. The question's unexpected, but it floods me with something like relief.

"Yeah, that sounds nice."

I smile, breathing in the eucalyptus scent of her hair, the smell already a memory of its own.

Hailey moves from me to Nolan, pulling him to her in a bear hug of an embrace. "How about you, want to join us?"

Nolan laughs, giving in to the hug for a second or two before extracting himself.

"No, thanks," he answers. "I've got plans."

Hailey smirks, nudging Nolan with her elbow.

"Yeah, so when am I going to meet him?" she asks.

Nolan's eyebrows shoot up beyond his fringe of hair, his cheeks tinging with pink.

"Uh, never?" he replies, embarrassed worry already in his words.

Hailey's good at being a big sister. With a look and a nudge, she's instilled more sibling terror than Thomas has provided all weekend. She's also managed to keep things peaceful, even though Nolan has every right to glower and storm away from her. I'm impressed she's so casual about what happened last night, and I'm astonished he is, too. More than anything, I'm happy they're not letting it be an excuse to keep their distance. Eli was wrong. We do learn from our parents' mistakes, at least some of the time.

"Oh, come on, what are you afraid of?" Hailey asks, fully aware of Nolan's discomfort and teasing him all the more for it. "What, is he hideously ugly or something?"

"Oh no, Brandon's gorgeous," Thomas says.

He slides behind Nolan, throwing an arm around his shoulder. Nolan's skin goes from pink to red in half a second flat, and I have to retract my thoughts about Thomas not embarrassing his little brother.

"Thomas!" Nolan groans, shrinking away from his arm.

Thomas grins, reaching up to ruffle his brother's hair.

"What? I may not be attracted to him, but that doesn't mean I can't appreciate his looks."

"Now I really have to meet him." Hailey laughs.

Nolan dives between the two, hurrying from the scene, probably to text his complaints to the subject of the conversation he's just ducked out of.

Thomas watches him leave, his smile softening.

"Can you two do me a favor?" he asks, once Nolan's a safe distance away.

"Sure, whatever you need," Hailey says.

"Keep an eye on him, okay?" Thomas murmurs, quiet enough his brother can't hear. "He's a big boy, and he can take care of himself. But still … keep an eye on him while I'm gone."

"You're really heading off this week?" Hailey asks.

She's been leaning into my side for the last half of this exchange, but now she pushes off of me and moves in to hug Thomas. He kisses the top of her head, and for a moment she keeps her face against his chest.

"Yeah." Thomas nods. "I'm going to drop Nolan off at home, and tomorrow I'll go over to Forrester's. We'll spend a few days cleaning up the apartment. Then we'll leave."

"Where are you going first?" I ask.

"To visit Julie's grave," Forrester answers, stepping over to us. "Even if she's not there, it seems like a good place to start the route Dad mapped out. And after we've finished that, we'll go west."

I don't know if I agree with Forrester skipping his final year of school to take this trip with Thomas. Going back after being away will be difficult, and he'll ruin his chances of getting anywhere decent in life if he doesn't have a high school diploma. But I see how much he needs this break. He's not shirking his responsibilities. He's clearing his head and reconnecting with family, too.

"We'll take care of Nolan," Hailey says, pulling away from Thomas to hug Forrester instead. "And you two make sure you stay in touch. I want emails, or texts. If you can't manage that, then send me a fucking postcard."

A billow of smoke sweeps across my face as I watch Hailey say goodbye to Forrester. My hair's going to smell like campfire when I'm home. Even once I've washed it, the smoky scent will stay.

Hailey says her goodbyes to Allison and Eli, extending the invitation for lunch to each of them. Allison says she has to work, but Eli — to my immense surprise — puts a note in his phone about it. I don't know if his heart is in the acceptance, but I appreciate the effort he's making to remember the date. Maybe things are not hopeless. Maybe even the twins will stay in touch after we've left today.

"I guess that's it," Hailey says as she steps back, her voice resigned.

She calls Star to her again as she fishes her keys out of her pocket. The rumble of a distant engine distracts me as Hailey gets into her car. Just as she turns the ignition, Dad's silver SUV pulls up alongside the twins' sporty ride.

"That's it for me, too," I say, turning from the car to collect my bags and start making my own round of goodbye hugs.

"Who's the cute driver?" Hailey asks, her head hanging out the open window.

I crinkle my nose and let out a snort of dismayed laughter.

"Um, my dad?" I tell her, glancing over my shoulder to see her quirking a brow at me.

"Unless we're living in a parallel universe, that's not your dad," she says before sticking her head back into the car and rolling the window up against the cold.

"What are you …"

I trail off, looking at the car to see someone much younger stepping out from the driver's seat. For far too many seconds, I'm confused, wondering if I've mistaken the car for a stranger's. But then the image of the young man before me clicks, and I break into a grin — and a run.

"Hudson?"

He stands by the door, looking shy and awkward, bright and beautiful.

"Hi," he says, his meek wave adorable.

I don't worry about our fight or his motivation for being here. I only run to him, sliding into his arms and breathing in the smell of his cologne. He hugs me back the way he hugged me the day he left, like he never wants to let me go. I press into him as much as I can, kissing his neck as he mumbles into my ear.

"I was stupid to get mad," he says, his lips warm against the skin of my earlobe — his body warm against the chill of the day. "I got home, and all I wanted was to see you. My parents kept going on about how nice it was to have the family together for Thanksgiving. But you're the family I want to spend my holiday with. Even if it's only for the drive home. Your dad said I could borrow his car. So I did."

We have plenty to talk about on the ride back to Aurora, and I have a lot to say in response to what he's just told me. Questions, answers. All of it will come, and soon. Because if nothing else, I've learned two things from this weekend. Holding on to the past is not possible, and even if it were possible, it would stunt our growth and inhibit our ability to live. But people who say that the past needs to be forgotten have it wrong, too. The past is, in its own way, a part of our present and our future. And just because we are different than we were a decade ago — or even a month ago — it doesn't mean we have to give up all things familiar, simply because they are old.

But for the moment, history — his, mine, and *ours* — can wait. For now, I only kiss him before turning back to my cousins to say my final goodbye.

No, not final. My temporary goodbye. My until-we-meet-again salute.

I get in my dad's car and take my boyfriend's hand as Hailey pulls out beside us. We wait until she completes a wide U-turn and speeds off down the road, and then we do the same.

ALLISON

Sunday, October 9th, 2016
41°F, overcast, 10 MPH winds — NW

Last night's storm was spectacular, both outside and in the cottage. I never imagined everyone else's lives could be as fractured as ours. Perhaps it's sadistic, but knowing we're not so far removed from the others is wonderful.

Going home now. Eli left right after Hailey and Kayla. He was anxious, like he couldn't wait to get away from this place. I worry about him. He's so wound up all the time. He never relaxes, never just lets things be.

Of course, he's been worse since he realized Dad was having an affair — worse still since he discovered I already knew about it. I thought about telling him. I thought about telling Mom, too. But what good would it do anyone? The world's an imperfect place. We got a big dose of that truth this weekend. I want to ask Dad about Julie, find out what side he was on. I want to know if he thought of her as a sister or as proof of the turmoil his family went through.

I hope he's smart enough not to get one of his flings pregnant. He has a main girl — I don't know her name, I've never bothered to ask — but not even Eli knows there are others, too. I just hope our father's sensible enough to keep all involved parties safe.

After we merged onto the highway, Dad told me he put an offer in on the cottage. He's always loved the place, but I didn't realize he'd be serious about snatching it up. I don't tell him Forrester is going to accept the offer this afternoon. He'll get the news soon enough.

If I know Dad, he's thinking a place like this would make a great hideaway for weekend trips with his girlfriends. I'd love to believe he wanted it out of fondness for the history he used to work so hard at preserving. But he's not the same person he used to be, and family has lost most of its meaningfulness to him. It's a shame, but who knows? Maybe one of us will pick up the role, help keep the legacy of our family alive.

And, hey, if he buys the cottage for his affair-house, at least it would mean something good came out of his bad behavior, right?

NOLAN

"EVERYTHING LOADED UP?" THOMAS asks as Forrester and I finish securing the tarp over the trailer.

The fire has been extinguished, the cottage is locked, and the day is so cold even the bay isn't tempting anymore. Runner dozes on the grass, and everyone else is gone. I'm antsy to head off as well. Thomas won't leave until Forrester's ready to go, though. Although honestly, I think he's been ready longer than the rest of us.

"We're done," Forrester says.

He nods, surveying the property around him. He seems unaffected, like he's only packing up for the day, not for good. But if I look hard enough, like if I damn near squint, I can see the pain. Forrester is hurting, and he will be for a long time. He's just not the type to get emotional, and I respect his quiet solemnity.

"That mean we're ready to leave?" I ask, trying to be patient but unable to hide the note of hope in my voice.

Thomas's smile is amused, though his eyes are disappointed. He wishes I cared more about this place. I know it's special for him, and I'm sad we don't share in the nostalgia. But I was too young, I guess. The difference between sixteen and nineteen doesn't feel all that great. But the difference between six and nine? Outstanding. My memories are far fewer, and my attachment is less.

Not that this property isn't awesome — I could easily fantasize about a beautiful summer sleepover here with Brandon — but since we're leaving for good, I don't see any point in trying to love the cottage now.

Forrester smirks at me, and then turns to my brother with a more meaningful smile.

"Tomorrow?" he asks, the question full of quiet, almost grim, excitement.

"Yeah, tomorrow." Thomas nods. "I'll come over early. I'll even bring breakfast. We'll clean up the apartment and get everything ready to go."

"Good," Forrester says. He calls to Runner, who I suppose will be the third companion on their adventure, before he walks toward his Jeep. "Thanks for all of this," he says, his back to us. "I should have thanked everyone. I ... I don't think I could have done all of this by myself."

"You don't have to thank us," Thomas says. "We understand."

Forrester lets out a soft breath of laughter as he faces us again.

"I know Julie's gone," he says. His expression is unclear, like he's not quite sure what he's even saying. "But we still gained a new family member this weekend. And, I mean, I get why it tore them apart. Even the ones on the same side of the fight ... I get it. But I still can't believe family is what broke the family up. After all this time. My dad missed his brothers. He missed all of you. We both did."

"We did, too," I say, which is not a declaration I expected to come out of my mouth, but one that feels right as I utter it.

"We're cousins, not brothers," Forrester continues, careful as he works through his thoughts, trying to pick the right words to say. "And cousins are different. But what happened to our dads. Let's ... let's not allow it to happen to us."

I don't have a response for that because I don't know any of my cousins well enough to agree.

"Let's not," Thomas says in my place, his assurance of our familial bond much stronger than mine.

Forrester nods and gives us a short wave. Then he opens the door for Runner to jump into the Jeep before he climbs in himself.

I'm excited to get home. But as we climb into our own car, I'm surprised to feel a touch of sadness knowing we're about to go. Maybe it's less about the cottage and more about my brother and his plans to leave home. He's old enough to move beyond our neighborhood, but that doesn't mean I'm not going to miss him and worry about him and wish he was around to be the stupidest — and wisest — person I know.

I won't argue with him on our way home. I planned to, until the canoe trip this morning. I expected to yell at him for abandoning Bea, even if the baby might not be his, even if she wants to have it with someone other than him.

But if Thomas's motives for leaving were aimless and self-centered at first, all that changed when he invited Forrester along.

Two years ago, my brother went missing for a week. I thought he was dead. I hoped he was only injured, even dreamed he'd suffered a head wound that would be scary but not as scary as having him gone for good. When he came home, unapologetic for his absence, I thought I'd never speak to him again for my fury. But then he told me the reason he went away — that one of his friends had given up on life, and so Thomas and a couple of others took the guy to the woods, shut themselves off from the outside world, and relaxed into nature until he was stable enough to come home and get help to keep himself going.

Forrester is not the same as that other guy. But he still needs help. He needs a friend and an escape from life for a while. Thomas will be his guide. And I think Forrester might help my brother figure out how to handle his own life, too.

I get in the car and don't even complain when Thomas rolls down the window, letting in the cold. For now, at least, I'm too busy getting out my phone to even notice as my brother starts the engine and puts the car in reverse.

Me: You'll never guess what.

B: You've won a million dollars?

Me: We're on our way home.

B: Even better.

THOMAS

I REMEMBER THE LAST time Nolan and I were here.

My brother inside, my cousin looking for our toys, and me floating in the water, listening to a conversation I'm not supposed to hear.

It makes no sense, and once Forrester is in the water, it drifts from my mind like a leaf blowing from branch to branch in a soft summer breeze.

A girl, a trip, a map. Two brothers regretting their past and making promises about their future.

I remember the last time Nolan and I were here.

But that time is no longer the last. This is the new final memory, and ten years from now, what will I retain from it?

Maybe Bea or Thanksgiving, maybe sitting in the dark living room talking to my cousins as storms raged outdoors and inside of us all.

Or maybe, my memory will be a simpler set of discoveries.

Like a girl, a trip, a map.

And two cousins, making more than promises about their future — making a pact that certain regrets will never reappear.

FORRESTER

TODAY IS NOT A good day.

Dad's dead. Cottage is gone.

This place has always been ours, but ours doesn't exist anymore, and now it's no longer even mine.

Today is not a good day.

This morning I discovered another relative gone. A death tore our family apart. But now a death has changed the path again. My *dad* has died. Only time will tell whether it'll have any effect on his brothers. But at least it's done something for their children. We weren't given a choice the first time. Family isn't so easy to break as my father and my uncles seemed to think.

I have my cousins again, and I won't lose them. *I won't lose them.* We might drift, sway, or float side by side. But I won't lose my family.

I sit in the Jeep for several minutes before I can bring myself to turn it on. Runner's already curled on the passenger seat, ready to snooze his way back to town. Me and Mom and Dad always made these drives together. Then it was just me and Dad. Now, this last time, it's just me.

Today is not a good day.

I flip the ignition and back the Jeep with its trailer of junk until I can turn the car around and head down the drive. Back to the roads. Back to the towns. Back to life without my father or my home.

I take a long look at the cottage as I drive past. Enough sun reflects off the windows to keep me from gazing inside one last time. I sigh, patting Runner's head as the cottage disappears from view. He doesn't care we're leaving. He might behave differently if he knew we're never coming back.

Today is not a good day.

Tonight, I'll be alone again. I won't sleep. Staying up is easier — lets me get a head start cleaning the apartment and packing my bags. Thomas will come in the morning, and when we're ready, he and I and Runner will take Julie's ashes and my dad's canoe. We'll load it all up, and then we'll just drive away.

Just drive away.

Just drive.

Away.

Today is not a good day.

But tomorrow ... tomorrow might be better.

MERE JOYCE has a Masters of Library and Information Science from the University of Western Ontario. She currently works as a librarian, and when she's not recommending great books to people, she's writing them. Her work includes *Shadow*, *Getting the Brush Off*, and *Blank Canvas*. Joyce lives in Kitchener, Ontario.

We acknowledge the sacred land on which Cormorant Books operates. It has been a site of human activity for 15,000 years. This land is the territory of the Huron-Wendat and Petun First Nations, the Seneca, and most recently, the Mississaugas of the Credit River. The territory was the subject of the Dish With One Spoon Wampum Belt Covenant, an agreement between the Iroquois Confederacy and Confederacy of the Ojibway and allied nations to peaceably share and steward the resources around the Great Lakes. Today, the meeting place of Toronto is still home to many Indigenous people from across Turtle Island. We are grateful to have the opportunity to work in the community, on this territory.

We are also mindful of broken covenants and the need to strive to make right with all our relations.